AUGUST

only 5 months left

D0099269

COUNT
DOWN

ANIEL PARKER

F   200036
PAR
PARKER, DANIEL
Count down: August $6.00

DATE DUE

OCT 29 '99			
MAR 30 '09			

"Death to the heretic!" Harold bellowed from the shadows. "Let the sacrifice begin!"

Julia bowed her head. Well, Luke finally got what he wanted. She nodded to herself. He always said that if she tried to run away from him, she would end up dead.

And look at me now.

But remarkably enough, even as a few kids stepped forward—eyes glazed, torches held high—Julia's fear and anger grew distant, fluttering away from her like a leaf on the wind.

Soon she would rest.

Memories of George washed over her in a soothing shower of images: the long drives alone, the carefree days in the cabin, the night after night of lying in each other's arms. . . .

I'll be with you again. Both of us will.

Yes. The three of them would be together for all eternity. She glanced down at the soft bulge of her womb, feeling calm and at peace. In a way, it was a blessing that George had never learned about their baby while he was alive. He had suffered so much already. It would have torn him apart. He had been better off not knowing.

"The flock will be pure from this day forward!" Harold cried. "Purged of lies and deceit! Nobody will ever stop us! Not even the Demon!"

The flames drew closer.

Julia closed her eyes and held her breath. *Please let it go quickly,* she prayed. *Please—*

About the Author

Daniel Parker is the author of over twenty books for children and young adults. He lives in New York City with his wife, a dog, and a psychotic cat named Bootsie. He is a Leo. When he isn't writing, he is tirelessly traveling the world on a doomed mission to achieve rock-and-roll stardom. As of this date, his musical credits include the composition of bluegrass sound-track numbers for the film *The Grave* (starring a bloated Anthony Michael Hall) and a brief stint performing live rap music to baffled Filipino audiences in Hong Kong. Mr. Parker once worked in a cheese shop. He was fired.

COUNT DOWN

AUGUST

by
Daniel Parker

Simon & Schuster

First Aladdin Paperbacks edition July 1999

Copyright © 1999 by 17th Street Productions,
a division of Daniel Weiss Associates, Inc.
and Daniel Ehrenhaft
Cover art copyright © 1999 by 17th Street Productions,
a division of Daniel Weiss Associates, Inc.

Produced by 17th Street Productions,
a division of Daniel Weiss Associates, Inc.
33 West 17th Street, New York, NY 10011

Cover design by Mike Rivilis

Aladdin Paperbacks
An imprint of Simon & Schuster
Children's Publishing Division
1230 Avenue of the Americas
New York, NY 10020

The text of this book was set in 10.5 point Rotis Serif.
Printed and bound in the United States of America
10 9 8 7 6 5 4 3 2 1

To Barbara and Michael

The Ancient Scroll
of the Scribes:

In the eighth lunar cycle,
During the months of Av and
Elul in the year 5759,
The most powerful among the Seers
will come eye to eye with the Chosen One.
He will arrive at the site of his visions,
The site of the Demon's ultimate wrath.
He stares out to sea on the high cliff,
Praying that the sand does not
slip through the hourglass,
Praying that the fire does
not slay his firstborn,
And the Chosen One is
blessed with a miracle.
Forsaken by the traitor, she breaks free.
But the Demon counterattacks with magic.

Each artery in the thin squid unseals a knife.
Eat sufficiently.
Then hunger is wasted on sport.
Eight twenty-six ninety-nine.

The countdown has started . . .

The long sleep is over.

For three thousand years I have patiently watched and waited. The Prophecies foretold the day when the sun would reach out and touch the earth—when my slumber would end, when my ancient weapon would breathe, when my dormant glory would blaze once more upon the planet and its people.

That day has arrived.

But there can be no triumph without a battle. Every civilization tells the same story. Good requires evil; redemption requires sin. The legends are as varied as are the civilizations that spawned them—yet each contains that same nugget of truth.

So I am not alone. The Chosen One awaits me. The flare opened the inner eyes of the Visionaries, those who can join the Chosen One to prevent my reign. But in order for them to defeat me, they must first make sense of their visions.

For you see, every vision is a piece of a puzzle, a puzzle that will eventually form a picture . . . a picture that I will shatter into a billion pieces and reshape in the image of my choosing.

I am prepared. My servants knew of this day. They made the necessary preparations to confuse the Visionaries—all in anticipation of that glorious time when the countdown ends and my ancient weapon ushers in the New Era.

My servants unleashed the plague that reduced the earth's population to a scattered horde of frightened adolescents. None of these children know how or why their elders and youngers perished.

And that was only the beginning.

My servants have descended upon the chaos. They will subvert the Prophecies in order to convert the masses into unknowing slaves. They will hunt down the Visionaries, one by one, until all are dead. They will eliminate the descendants of the Scribes so that none of the Visionaries will learn of the scroll. The hidden codes shall remain hidden. Terrible calamities and natural disasters will wreak havoc upon the earth. Even the Chosen One will be helpless against me.

I *will* triumph.

PART I:

August 1, 1999

**Wilderness near Strizhi,
Russia
4:45 P.M.**

The boy's arm always tingled before a storm.

There were other signs of rain, too, of course—the brisk wind, the ominous clouds to the west. But the pain that stretched from his left elbow to his fingertips meant that the rain would start very soon. The boy paused for a moment and scanned the rocky hillside. There was probably a cave hidden somewhere in the bushes—

"Smotri, vot kakaya-ta berluga," a gruff voice called from over the crest of a small ridge.

The boy drew in his breath. Once again he had fallen behind Misha and the girls. He hurried to catch up with them, swatting branches out of his face as he ran uphill. It seemed as if his entire life had been a continuous struggle to keep up with Misha, Ilya, and Svetla—or simply to *communicate* with them, to understand their strange language.

His bony wrist throbbed. Had there ever been a time when he wasn't in pain? When he wasn't exhausted? Or hungry? Or confused?

No. And no matter how hard he fought to remember anything before these months of incessant travel, his memory would only take him so far . . . back to the same impenetrable wall of nothingness.

"*Karatyshka!*" the voice shouted.

I'm going as fast as I can, the boy thought. He gritted his teeth. Misha never stopped barking orders at him. At least he had learned enough bits and pieces of Misha's language to know that "*Karatyshka*" was *not* his name. It was an insult. It meant "runt." *So what is my name?* the boy wondered again—as he did a dozen times every day. He shook his head and stumbled up onto the level dirt of the ridge.

"*Ostorozhno,*" Misha growled. He grabbed the boy's arm to steady him, but the boy shook free of his grasp.

Their eyes met for a moment. Even after all this time, something in Misha's face still made the boy uneasy—the penetrating black pupils, the hard angles of his chin and nose, the dark hair. He looked like some kind of predatory bird. The boy much preferred to rest his gaze on the soft, plump, white faces of the sisters: Ilya and Svetla. At least they knew how to smile. *They* made him feel at home. They always had. His first clear memory was of their hovering over his body, bandaging his broken arm and ministering to his mysterious wounds like two angels. . . .

Misha jerked his finger toward a dark crevice in a sheer wall of bedrock on the side of the ridge.

The boy nodded. So there *was* a cave. Good. He peered at it closely.

Wait a second. Was that a wisp of smoke floating out of it?

Ilya sniffed the air. *"Pozhar,"* she said.

The boy's eyes narrowed. *Pozhar* was their word for "fire"— that much he knew. That meant the cave was probably occupied. He turned to Misha, who shrugged.

A few drops of rain splattered in the dirt.

Misha strode toward the entrance. Ilya and Svetla exchanged a quick glance, but they followed silently in his footsteps.

The boy hesitated. The rain intensified, pattering on his head and shoulders, washing his long black bangs down in front of his eyes. He brushed his hair aside. Was this such a great idea? Maybe they should just keep going. The storm wasn't so bad yet. . . .

Misha paused just outside the cave. *"Ostorozhno,"* he hissed again.

The boy swallowed. Why were the four of them continually stumbling into traps? Hadn't they learned anything? Hardly a week passed when they didn't walk into some village or hut or forest—only to find themselves being attacked by a crazed gang of starving teenagers. And as he forced himself to approach the cave, he wondered: *Was life always like this?* Somehow he didn't think it was. Somehow he was certain that the world had once been very different. But so long as he couldn't remember any details, there was no way he could know for sure. Misha and the girls certainly couldn't tell him.

The thick, pungent smell of burning wood grew stronger as the boy drew closer.

He could see the smoke quite clearly now, a pale cloud drifting over the heads of the others.

7

"Going in there is really stupid, you know that?" he muttered. He knew full well that they couldn't understand a word he was saying.

The three of them gazed back at him and shrugged. Then they turned and ducked through the narrow chasm, vanishing into the smoke-filled darkness.

The boy shook his head. *Stupid,* he repeated to himself.

Still, he crouched low and crept after them, feeling his way into the cave by running his hands along the damp stone walls. As much as it frightened him to enter this place, the thought of being left alone—even for a few moments—was far more terrifying. His fear of abandonment was what bound him to these three. And they knew it.

"Strasviture?" Misha called. His voice reverberated in the dank blackness.

There was no answer.

The boy heard a scraping sound, glimpsed a flash of red. Misha was lighting a torch.

Gradually the cave took shape in the dim, orange light. It was very narrow—barely wide enough for one person. The boy's eyes began to smart. The smoke was quite thick. His head swam as he inched forward, directly behind Svetla. The air was really thin in here—

"Bozhe moi!" Misha cried.

Svetla jerked to a stop.

The boy nearly slammed into her. *Something's wrong.* He glanced over his shoulder.

The cave entrance suddenly seemed far away—a dim, gray sliver of rain.

"What is it?" the boy whispered, whirling back toward Misha. He craned his neck in an effort to see past the two girls and bumped his head on the slimy stone roof. "What's wrong?"

"*Chert voz'mi!*" Misha called.

Svetla scuttled toward the torchlight. The boy crawled after her. His heart began to pound. At least Misha didn't sound scared. No, if anything, Misha sounded *excited*. That was a good sign, wasn't it?

"*Karatyshka,*" Misha urged. "*Karatyshka . . .*"

Almost before he even knew it, the boy found himself in a vast, open space.

My God.

He straightened and dusted himself off, then took a look around.

The cave was *huge*. The smoldering remnants of the fire sat glowing and belching smoke in the middle of the floor, maybe twenty paces away. The boy shook his head. No wonder people sought shelter in here. The ceiling was so high, he couldn't even see it. And the walls—

The walls!

They were covered with black drawings. Dozens of them. Maybe hundreds. Even in the uncertain, flickering light of Misha's torch, the boy could see that every single visible square inch had been splashed with graffiti.

A strange heat filled his chest.

What is this place?

It reminded him of something—something from the distant past—but he couldn't quite place it. Misha brought the flame close to the image of what looked like a face. The boy took a step forward. The sensation in his chest grew more powerful, almost painful. The face was undeniably human, but it was unlike any the boy had ever seen: lined, sagging, and sickly . . . with huge bags below the eyes and a long, flowing beard.

Why was it so familiar? *Why?*

"Starik," Misha whispered. His voice quavered.

The two girls huddled around him, shaking their heads, gaping.

The boy bit his lip. His heart was racing now; his mouth was very dry. He took a step forward. Never before had he felt so *close* to figuring something out. That face . . . Its meaning hovered on the edges of his consciousness. He *knew* it. It was as if the key to unlocking his past were encoded in that drawing—and all he had to do was look at it a certain way, and then he'd be able to . . . he'd be able to . . .

A scream split the stagnant air.

The boy jerked. Panic seized him. It was Svetla. His eyes widened in horror as she pressed her hands against the sides of her head, then collapsed in a heap on the hard cave floor.

"Chuma!" Misha cried.

The boy's knees buckled. *Chuma.* He knew what that meant. Of all the phrases in his companions' strange tongue, he'd understood that one from the beginning. *Chuma* was their term for the disease—the horrible sickness that struck older kids without warning and reduced them to puddles of black slime. He'd seen it happen hundreds of times on their travels. Only for some reason, he'd never expected it to happen to one of *them.*

"Svetla!" Ilya shrieked, falling to her knees beside the crumpled body. "Svetla!"

Misha whirled around frantically—one way, then the other.

Do something! an inner voice commanded the boy. But he only stood and stared. There was nothing he *could* do. Svetla began to writhe on her back, howling in agony. Black welts appeared on her face. It would be over in a matter of seconds—

"C'est la mort!" a raspy voice barked from the shadows.

A figure dashed out of the darkness beyond the fire and shoved Ilya out of the way—then crouched beside Svetla and grabbed her head. The boy couldn't react. He couldn't even scream. The figure was stuffing something into Svetla's throat. Svetla struggled. *That person is killing her!* She kicked once, arms flailing wildly . . . then abruptly relaxed.

The cave was perfectly silent, save for the faint crackling of the torch.

The boy held his breath. Svetla lay still. She twitched once, then opened her eyes. The disease . . . it had stopped. She hadn't melted. The boy had never seen anything like it. Everybody knew that the disease was incurable. It was part of life. When a person approached his or her twenty-first birthday, a person died. *Every* person. No exceptions. The boy's unbelieving eyes flashed to Misha. His face was a ghostly white, but the faint beginnings of a smile appeared on his trembling lips.

"Svetla?" he murmured. "Svetla?"

She nodded. "Misha?" she croaked.

11

"Svetla!" the boy found himself crying.

Everyone turned to him at once—including the mysterious figure.

The boy gasped.

The figure was a man.

And his face was identical to the face in the drawing.

The boy shuddered in a rush of wonderment and fear as his eyes absorbed every wrinkle in the man's gaunt, bearded face. *That's it. That's what I couldn't understand,* the boy realized. *This man . . . he's* old.

**Amarillo,
Texas
11:40 A.M.**

Of all the bizarre and sickening things that had happened to George Porter since New Year's Eve, he never once imagined he'd have to scrounge through Harold Wurf's bedroom for a pair of pants.

He was dressing in *Harold's* clothes. Just thinking about it made him ill.

Then again, compared to some other stuff he'd seen and done, this was nothing. Less than nothing. He'd watched a thousand kids turn to black glop. He'd nearly drowned. He'd crawled through a sewer to fake his own death, for God's sake—then spent the next month living in the woods like a wild dog, eating insects and tree bark just to stay alive.

But right now . . . well, he kind of felt like puking.

Socks and underpants flew as he rifled through drawer after drawer. He was starting to get pissed. He paused for a moment and stared at himself in the closet mirror—wearing nothing but a lame T-shirt and dorky polka-dot boxer shorts.

I look like Harold.

No doubt about it. He nodded, scowling at his reflection through his stringy blond bangs. His

13

green eyes hardened. *I look like the lunatic who locked me up and stole my girlfriend from me. I look like that smooth-talking son of a bitch who fooled all those Visionaries into thinking that he was the real Chosen One—*

Okay. He needed to chill. So what if he looked like Harold? It didn't *mean* anything. Throwing a fit was pointless. He had to find some clothes, and these were the only ones available. He'd wasted plenty of anger on Harold already. Now he had to *act*—to pack up what supplies he could and get the hell out of here, to track Julia down and take her back.

He took a deep breath and glanced down at the battered wooden bureau. It was practically empty. *Crap.* There was nothing in here. Nothing. What kind of a room *was* this? Didn't the guy own any pants at all?

Maybe George should skip the pants altogether and wear boxers. Boxer shorts weren't much different than regular shorts, right? Besides, it was really hot outside. It was the height of summer. He was already sweating. But those two chicks downstairs might get a little freaked out if he strutted around in his underwear. He grinned slightly. He could tell they already thought he was weird. Then again, he couldn't exactly blame them. They'd walked onto Harold's farm, expecting to find a false prophet and a promised land . . . and instead they'd found *him*— alone in the kitchen, dirty and starving, scarfing down a jar of grape jelly.

Some welcoming committee, huh?

He laughed out loud. Now that he thought about

it, he really shouldn't care *what* those girls thought. Nope. Anyway, *they* were the weird ones.

Like that one chick, Sarah, the brunette with the glasses—she'd hardly said a word to him since they'd showed up a week ago. And the other one, the redhead . . . what was her name? Aviva? She was getting on his nerves. She kept going on about how her visions were driving her crazy, that she had to go west, that George had to get off his butt and find a car as soon as possible.

Didn't she understand that *he* was a Visionary, too? He felt the same pull out west that she did. He knew that they had to move. The problem was that he was *sick*. He could hardly stand. He'd barely slept or eaten in a month. And he wasn't about to leave before he was strong and clearheaded enough to look for Harold. No way. He needed all his wits about him.

Those two girls didn't have the slightest clue what they would be dealing with.

They had no idea how Harold could fool anyone with slick double-talk, how he could pull off miracle after phony miracle. But that wasn't even what worried George most.

No. What worried him most was the Demon.

The Demon was responsible for Harold's power. George knew that now. The Demon was using her magic to make Harold look like some kind of god. There was no other way Harold could have possibly done that crap: the healings, the locusts, any of it.

Maybe George should skip going after Harold. Yeah. Maybe it wasn't so smart to look for Julia. He knew he didn't have much time. The pull had never been stronger. If Julia just followed her own visions, they would take her to the same place he was going—

"Hey, George?" a small voice called from the hallway. "Can I come in?"

George swallowed. "Uh . . . yeah," he answered.

The door creaked open. Aviva stepped into the room. She smiled at George, then blushed and lowered her eyes. "I'm, uh . . . I'm sorry," she stammered. "I can come back later when you're, uh, dressed."

Oh, brother. He glanced down at himself. Now she probably thought he was some kind of pervert. "It's all right," he grumbled. "I can't find any pants, anyway."

He shook his head. It was funny. He couldn't help but remember that time when he'd caught Julia in her underwear, all those months ago . . . in that log cabin in Illinois. Only then *he* was the one who'd turned red. A twinge of emptiness shot through him. She'd been so cool about it. She'd been *flattered* that he was staring at her legs. He'd never been more happy than he was in that place at that moment. *Never.* Even *before* the plague. That was the night he'd first confessed his feelings for her. It was the night they'd first made love. He could picture every last detail. . . .

". . . you all right?" Aviva was asking.

He jerked his head up. "Huh?"

She smiled again, blinking shyly at him from behind her red curls. "You seem a little preoccupied. Are you okay?"

"Fine," he muttered. He frowned and turned back to the bureau. He noticed that her big, ugly knapsack was leaning against it. Maybe *that's* what she wanted. "So what's up? You want your stuff?"

"No," she murmured. "I just came to see if you wanted some company."

"I'm used to being alone," he said with a grunt.

She didn't say anything. He heard her footsteps, then felt something on his back—the light tickle of fingers.

"Hey!" he barked, flinching away from her. Why was she sneaking up on him like that? Couldn't she tell that he was tense?

"George, I'm sorry," she whispered, shaking her head. "I didn't mean to scare you."

He took a step back, and his butt knocked against the open drawers. She was standing so damn *close* all of a sudden.

"What do you *want?*" he demanded.

"I just wanted to see if you were lonely," she whispered.

His eyes narrowed. *Lonely?* What was she talking about? Aviva never acted like this. Usually she sat around and whined. Either that or she got on his case about leaving. Maybe she'd decided to break into Harold's parents' liquor cabinet.

"I'm *fine,*" he repeated. "And if you came to bug me about getting out of here, I'm almost ready. I just need to find some clothes. All of mine got ruined when I—"

"I didn't come up here to bug you," she interrupted. Her voice was low, husky. She drew closer, trapping George between the bureau and her body. Her face was only about a foot away from his own. "I came for something else."

17

George bit his lip. He almost felt like laughing. This chick *must* be drunk—or stoned, or *something*. Was she serious?

"What's the matter?" she asked softly.

"You tell *me*," he mumbled. "No offense, but would you mind backing off a little bit?"

She raised her eyebrows. "Do you really want me to?" She reached out and ran her hand through his tangled mop of hair. "I was just thinking—"

"That's enough," he snarled, swatting her arm aside. "I have a girlfriend. I *told* you that, remember?"

"A girlfriend?" She threw back her head and laughed. "What does that have to do with anything?"

George's jaw tightened. "It has to do with the fact that I'm in love with *her*, not you. Now I'm not gonna ask you again. *Back off*. Take your bag and get out of here."

She teasingly pursed her lips. "You don't find me attractive?"

"*What?*" He shook his head, flabbergasted. "Uh, well, *no*—but that's not even the point. It's just . . . it's, like, eleven o'clock in the morning. We're getting ready to leave. I mean, what's Sarah doing right now?"

Aviva groaned and rolled her eyes. "She's asleep, George. She won't hear a thing."

George blinked. In spite of the fact that he was growing increasingly ticked off, he had to laugh. Nobody was *this* horny. It was ridiculous. Did she honestly believe he would fool around with her? So what if Sarah was asleep? That had nothing to do with anything.

"Listen, George," Aviva stated. Her tone changed. All at once she sounded very businesslike. "Have you ever wondered what's happening to the world?"

George didn't answer. His smile faded.

What's happening to the world?

Somebody had asked him that same question once before: another weird chick—back in February, in some little crap town in Ohio. Her name was Amanda.

She tried to kill him.

She wanted him dead because he was a Visionary. She worshiped the Demon, and so did all the other girls she hung out with.

"I mean, I know you have," Aviva went on in the silence. "You're a Visionary. But what's the point in wondering? Do you really think we're going to figure out what's happening? Will we be able to stop it? Probably not. We're all going to end up melting, just like everyone else. So I have a philosophy. We should all just get our kicks while we can. . . ."

No, no, no.

George's blood ran cold. He couldn't listen anymore.

Aviva was repeating everything Amanda had said. Exactly. *Word for word.* There was no denying it; he could never forget Amanda's little speech even if he *wanted* to forget it. It was burned into his memory.

And Amanda had been hitting on him when she'd delivered it—just the way Aviva was now.

It couldn't be a coincidence.

No. He was in danger. Aviva and Sarah were Demon worshipers, too. He'd known something was wrong with them.

Make a move!

19

"Don't you agree?" Aviva whispered, leaning toward him.

George's eyes frantically darted around the room. There was a lamp on the dresser—big, old-fashioned, with a heavy, metal base. She was so close now; he could feel her breath on his cheek. His brain seemed to fill with a hot, white haze. His heart thundered in his rib cage. In a flash he spun away from her, seized the lamp with both hands—and lifted it high over his head.

"George!" she cried. "What—"

He smashed the lamp down on top of her skull. It struck with a sharp *crack*.

Aviva let out a bloodcurdling scream.

George winced. Blood spewed from the top of her head, and she dropped to her knees.

"Aviva?" The word floated up from somewhere downstairs. "Are you okay?"

No time to waste. George was breathing heavily now. He flung the lamp aside and grasped Aviva's neck, squeezing the soft flesh until his fingers met. He stared down at the bloody gash on her scalp. She fought to look at him, her face turning red. Her eyes bulged.

Footsteps thumped up the stairs.

"Let . . . go . . . of . . . me," Aviva choked. Her face turned from red to purple. She scratched his hands with her fingernails. George ignored the pain. He had to finish off Aviva before Sarah could stop him. Nobody was going to prevent him from getting out of here and seeing Julia again. *Nobody.* He gripped her harder, grinding his teeth.

20

"No!" a voice shouted just outside the open door. "What are you *doing?*"

Aviva clawed at him desperately. George held his breath. She was losing strength—he could feel it. She was turning blue. Just a few more seconds . . .

"Stop it!" the voice in the hall shrieked.

Finally Aviva's arms flopped to the floor.

Her head lolled to one side. Her eyes remained open, staring at nothing.

One down, one to go.

"What have you done? My God . . . What have you *done?"*

George exhaled, then looked toward the doorway.

Sarah was staring at him, her face a ghastly white. She was shivering uncontrollably. But he didn't feel anything—no fear, or remorse, or even shock at the fact that he had actually *killed* somebody.

No.

All he felt was hatred. Hatred for the Demon. But most of all, hatred for the Demon's servants—these girls that stalked him at every turn and ruined what little life he had left.

"You're dead, too, Sarah," he gasped. *"Dead."*

187 Puget Drive,
Babylon, Washington
9:45 A.M.

Ariel sat on the edge of her rumpled bed, blearily squinting through the window at the bright blue sky. She couldn't remember the last time she'd been up so early on a Sunday. Well, no, that wasn't quite true. She'd watched the sunrise plenty of times—but it was always after a long night of partying. So those mornings didn't really count. Everybody knew that Sunday didn't officially start until a person actually went to sleep, no matter *what* time it was.

Then again, she hadn't slept in days.

So maybe it was still Saturday night. Maybe there was still time to go back to the mall and undo what had happened, to start over so everything would be cool . . . and then she would go to bed, and when she woke up, her life would be back to normal—

"Try to get some rest," Leslie murmured.

"I can't," Ariel croaked.

She sounded like a frog. But it figured. She'd spent the last ten hours bawling, pretty much non-stop.

"Look, Ariel, we *know* it isn't true. So why does it bother you so much?"

23

Ariel took a deep breath and rubbed her bloodshot hazel eyes, then glanced back at Leslie. *Man.* Even after an all-nighter—a very *trying* all-nighter—Leslie still looked fresh and beautiful. She was sprawled across the mattress with her head propped up against some pillows. How did she *do* it, anyway? Leslie Tisch could run a marathon and go boozing for ten hours, and she'd still be fit to model for a Victoria's Secret catalog.

"Well?" Leslie pressed. "Why?"

"It bothers me because I can't remember," Ariel finally muttered.

"Of course you can't!" Leslie cried, sitting up straight. She tossed her long black curls over her shoulders. "It was a totally traumatic event. Your mother *died*, Ariel. You saw the accident. Think about it. I mean, you're the one who's always going on about that psych class you took. So you know what happens after people suffer a traumatic event."

Ariel sniffed. "What?"

"They *forget* about it," Leslie replied with a reassuring smile. "They repress the memory."

Maybe. Ariel just sat there, gazing into Leslie's dark, saucer-shaped eyes. She knew exactly what Leslie was talking about, of course. And she *had* considered the possibility that she'd repressed the memory. But it wasn't a very comforting thought. Because if that were true, it would mean that something so devastating had happened that she couldn't even face it. She *could* face her mother's death, though. Couldn't she? It hurt, but she could do it. After all, she remembered the funeral. She remembered the

24

events *surrounding* the death very clearly. She just couldn't remember the death itself. . . .

"There's no way you could have hurt your own mother," Leslie stated. She leaned forward and draped her arm around Ariel's slumped shoulders. "I know it."

"How?" Ariel whispered. Her throat caught. *Uh-oh.* Now she would probably start sobbing again. "How do you know?"

"Because you're a good person," Leslie whispered. "Because you've got a pure soul."

A pure soul? Ariel almost laughed. Those were definitely *not* the words she'd use. Even describing her soul as "semipolluted" would be a stretch. No, she was a conniving, scheming, self-centered bitch—and she knew it. Yup. She knew it way before last night, too. Way before Trevor accused her of murdering their mother, way before people started melting whenever they got within ten feet of her . . . even way before the blackout and the plague. She'd *always* known it. Her acute self-awareness was her greatest strength. It was also the key to her popularity. Her *former* popularity, anyway.

"I'm your friend, Ariel," Leslie added. "I wouldn't lie to you."

Ariel swallowed. The lump in her throat swelled. She couldn't speak. If she didn't have Leslie . . . Well, she didn't want to think about that.

Everybody in Babylon hates me.

It was true. And they would all hear about what happened. Everyone would hear that Ariel was a monster who had killed her own mom when she was

25

seven years old. Jezebel would tell them. There was no doubt in Ariel's mind about *that*. Jez was probably already spreading the word. She must have known Trevor was going to pull something at the mall last night. For all Ariel knew, Jezebel had even orchestrated the whole thing. Why else would she be waiting there? Why else would she have brought Ariel's boyfriend, Caleb? Judging from that creamy look of satisfaction in her eyes when Trevor started crying . . .

Jezebel.

Ariel's stomach squeezed. Only eight months ago—eight measly months, not even a whole *year*— Jezebel had sworn that she loved Ariel, that the two of them would be friends forever, that they were "family."

Yeah. Some family.

Maybe Ariel *hadn't* been so popular as she would like to believe. Maybe people had always hated her. It was pretty obvious that Jezebel had. Jez was just too scared to admit it. Wouldn't it be reasonable to assume that everyone else felt the same way? Maybe all those Chosen One freaks were right about her—that there was something wrong with her, that she was *evil*. Finding out about her mother was only the first step in discovering who she really was.

Who knew what other horrors lay buried beneath the surface?

"Can I ask you something, Leslie?" she found herself saying. Her voice was strained. "Have *you* ever repressed something bad?"

Leslie gave Ariel's shoulder a gentle squeeze.

"No," she murmured. "But I know people who have."

Great, Ariel thought miserably. She bowed her head. Never before had she so desperately wished she were somebody else—*anybody* else. Like Leslie. God, wouldn't it be nice to trade places with her? Not only would Ariel be free of her own dismal existence, but she could exchange her booze-addled body and drab brownish blond hair for that perfect skin and those long curls—

"Hey!" Leslie suddenly cried. She slapped her palm against her forehead. "Duh. I'm so stupid. We can make *sure* that you didn't kill your mother."

Ariel glanced up at her, frowning. "How?"

Leslie flashed a sly grin. "I can hypnotize you."

"Uh . . . sorry. My sense of humor isn't what it used to be."

"I mean it," Leslie insisted. "Seriously. I learned how to do it back in Portland. A hypnotist came to an assembly at my high school and put on this awesome show. He brought all these kids onstage and got them to say all this funny stuff. . . . Anyway, I signed up for a course." She sat up straight and smiled proudly. "I'm a fully certified hypnotist."

Ariel blinked. "You have *got* to be kidding me."

"It's the truth." Leslie shrugged, then hopped off the bed and peered at the heaps of clothing and garbage on Ariel's purple shag carpet. "I just need a lighter."

In spite of herself Ariel started to smile. Who else but Leslie would ever become a certified hypnotist?

"I don't know about this," Ariel mumbled sarcastically. "I might have to see some credentials. Do you have a license on you?"

"It's back in Portland," Leslie answered, without a trace of irony. She glanced back at Ariel. "Come on, I'm *serious*. Do you have a lighter or not?"

"In the top drawer of the desk," Ariel said. She shook her head. She couldn't believe she would actually go through with something like this. . . .

Leslie yanked open the drawer and rummaged through it for a moment before pulling out a green Bic. "Aha!" She flicked the igniter, and a small flame appeared. "Perfect." She beamed at Ariel, then pulled out her desk chair and sat facing her. "Now lie back and relax."

"Uh . . . this isn't dangerous or anything, is it?" Ariel asked. "I mean, it's not the kind of thing where I can fall asleep and never wake up, right?"

Leslie cocked her eyebrow. "It's a lot less dangerous than chugging beer out of a funnel," she said dryly. "Now lie down."

Ariel smirked, but she eased back against the pillows.

What was the worst that could happen? Actually, she didn't want to answer that question. Better to focus on the positives. Yes. Ariel Collins: Miz Positivity. She couldn't forget that. The *best* that could happen was that she'd remember her mother's accident and that Trevor would be proved wrong—and that Caleb would see she *wasn't* the lowest form of scum ever to walk the planet . . . and so on and so forth, until she ruled the Babylon social scene once again.

Oh, yeah. Sure. And maybe the Chosen One freaks will build a statue in my honor.

"Just make yourself as comfortable as possible,"

28

Leslie instructed. She scooted up to the edge of the bed and held the lighter in front of Ariel. "Clear your mind and concentrate on the flame."

Ariel took a deep breath and stared at the tiny, dancing light.

"I want you to listen carefully to the sound of my voice."

Ariel nodded.

"You are totally relaxed," Leslie went on. "Your body is warm and comfortable."

Much to Ariel's surprise, she *did* feel pretty relaxed. The way Leslie was talking . . . It was smooth and soothing, like a mellow song.

The flame flickered—a glowing arch of yellow and red.

"I'm going to start counting down from ten," Leslie said. Her droning voice seemed to fill the entire room. "When I reach one, you will be in a deep sleep. Ten . . . nine . . . You are comfortably tired. Your eyelids are very heavy."

Ariel's vision grew fuzzy. The pulsating light grew in size, but dimmed at the same time.

"Eight . . . seven . . . six . . . You are slipping out of consciousness. . . ."

I think I'll just rest my eyes for a minute, Ariel thought.

The flame fluttered, then disappeared. A pleasant numbness filled her body.

"Five . . . four . . . three . . . You are almost asleep. You feel very calm, very peaceful."

Leslie's disembodied voice covered her like a warm blanket.

"Two . . . one . . ."

29

"Ariel? Ariel, honey? Are you almost ready?"

Mommy is calling. I better go get dressed. But I don't want to leave.

Why not?

Because I want to stay at home. Mommy and Daddy always make us go to church on Sundays. I'd rather watch TV and play with Trevor. Other kids get to stay at home. Jezebel never has to go to church.

Why don't you like church?

It's boring. I always fall asleep.

"Ariel? Come on, Moey, be a good girl and get ready," *Mommy calls again. I like when she calls me Moey—she says it was her mother's pet name for her, too.*

How do you answer Mommy?

I go to the bathroom and knock on the door. She's taking a bath. She always takes a bath before church. She likes to be clean.

And then what happens?

I open the door . . . and Mommy is washing herself. She has her hair in one of those plastic caps. It's funny.

Why?

I don't know. It looks funny. But she isn't laughing. She wants me to get ready. I don't like it when Mommy's mad. I want her to laugh. So I run over and grab the cap off her head.

What does she do?

She's a little mad, but I can tell she thinks it's sort of funny. She laughs a little bit. So I run back to the tub and splash her hair. Now we can't go to church!

What happens next?

I don't . . . I don't know. It's bad. I can't . . .

It's okay, Ariel. You're perfectly safe. Nothing can harm you. These are only memories. What happens next?

She says she has to dry her hair now.

And then?

She's really mad. I didn't want her to be that mad. I want to help. So I . . . I . . .

Remember, Ariel—you're safe. You're very comfortable.

I get her hair dryer. It looks like a big toy gun. I tell her I'll help! I'll dry her hair for her while she takes a bath. That way she can save time. I've seen her dry her hair before. I know how to do it. I'm a big girl.

Do you dry her hair?

I plug it in. . . . The plug is high. I have to stand on my tippy toes. Mommy keeps telling me, "No, no. Don't do that." She's still mad. I don't want her to be mad.

But you don't listen?

I want to help. I plug it in and I bring it over to the tub. I point it at her hair. She's yelling at me now. She's trying to stand up, but her foot slips. I've never seen her so mad. All I want to do is help. Then she'll stop being mad.

You're sure you want to help?

Yes! That's why I'm doing it. She tells me to turn it off right away, but I blast her hair with the dryer. I'm helping. And then . . . and then . . .

Go on, Ariel.

The dryer slips.

It slips? Or do you drop it?

31

It slips! It falls in the tub. I was just playing. I didn't mean it! No! It's so bad . . . so bad . . . Mommy is screaming, and there's this noise. . . . I can't stand the noise. I can hear it! It's buzzing. I press my hands over my ears and squeeze my eyes shut. I tell her I'm sorry, I'm sorry, and Daddy and Trevor come in, and I see Trevor—

Ariel's eyes popped open. She lay on her bed, gasping for breath. It was over. There was a sharp pain in her palms. She glanced down at her hands—and saw that her nails were digging into her own flesh.

"You're awake now, Ariel," Leslie breathed. "Are you okay?"

"Uh . . . not really," she whispered shakily. She looked up at Leslie.

Oh, my—

Leslie wasn't alone.

Caleb stood beside her. He stared down at Ariel, shaking his head. His eyes were wide under his mop of messy brown bangs. His broad lips were quivering.

"Trevor was right," he murmured. "He was *right.*"

No! Ariel opened her mouth—but before she could say a word, Caleb bolted out of the room and slammed the door behind him.

CHAPTER FOUR

Amarillo,
Texas
12:50 P.M.

"I swear, George, I don't know what you're talking
about," Sarah whispered. "Please. Just take it easy. . . ."

George took a step closer.

Help me. Sarah's eyes remained pinned to the
bloody, broken lamp in George's hands. There was no
way she could escape. Her back was jammed against
the door at the end of the narrow hall—and *he*
blocked the only path downstairs. Maybe if she just
lunged at him . . .

"You worship the Demon," George growled. "Just
like those chicks in Ohio. You came here to kill me.
Harold sent you. Right? Didn't he?"

Sarah swallowed. *Chicks in Ohio?* Nothing George
said made any sense. He was babbling. Something in
his brain had snapped. But she should have expected
it. The poor kid had spent the last month pretending
to be dead, fighting for survival in the wilderness—
alone, cut off from everyone and everything. He was
bound to be paranoid. He was *bound* to go insane.
The only surprise was that it hadn't happened
sooner—

"Answer me!" he barked.

33

"I told you, I've never met this Harold person," Sarah whispered. She felt as if she were listening to someone else, a stranger. Her voice quivered so much that it was unrecognizable to herself. "I don't know anything about what happened in Ohio. But if you—"

"Liar!" he interrupted.

Sarah winced. If he took another step, he'd be within striking distance. There *had* to be some way to stop him. She was the Chosen One. A miracle always saved her. Without fail. Where was the magic now? What could she possibly *do?* Maybe she should just tell him the truth. But no . . . The last time she'd told somebody she was the Chosen One, she'd been thrown out of a car and left for dead in the snow. What other options did she have? *Think!*

"I'm gonna give you one last chance to answer me before I kill you," George stated in a dead voice. He inched forward, his green eyes boring into her own. "Either you tell me who you are and what you want—or you're gonna die in the next ten seconds."

"You—you might not believe me if I told you," she found herself stammering.

His eyes narrowed. "What the hell is *that* supposed to mean?" Sarah bit her lip. "Okay, George, look. I'm the Chosen One. Aviva was the only person left alive who knew. I was waiting to tell you until we caught up with the False Prophet." The words exploded from her mouth in a jumble; she spoke so fast, she hardly knew what she was saying. "Maybe those girls in Ohio are hooked up with these girls in black robes, the servants of the Demon—"

"Shut up," he snapped. *"You're* the Chosen One?

34

And you actually think I'm gonna *believe* you? How stupid do you think I am?"

The fear pulsating through Sarah's body began to turn to panic. She started trembling. Her thoughts clouded. "Listen . . . just—just wait, okay? Just tell me what Aviva did. What did she do to make you want to hurt us?"

"You know damn well what she did."

Sarah shook her head violently. "No, I don't, George. But whatever it was, I'm sure it was a mistake. I *know* Aviva. We've been together for months. Just the two of us. We're not dangerous. We don't have any weapons, or black robes, or *anything.*" Her voice rose. "Just look through our stuff. See for yourself. Go open Aviva's knapsack. I'm serious."

George hesitated. He glanced over his shoulder at the open bedroom door, then back at Sarah. "Why should I do that? How do I know something isn't gonna jump out at me?"

"Okay—let *me* do it," she pleaded desperately.

For a moment George stared at her. Then he lowered his gaze, as if studying the makeshift club in his hands . . . as if debating whether or not to use it.

Please, George.

"Okay," he finally whispered. "I'll let you open your friend's knapsack. And if there aren't any answers in there, I'm gonna smash this lamp over your head, same as I did to her." He glanced at her again. "How does that sound?"

"Okay," she croaked. "Okay." She swallowed and held up her hands, palms facing him, very carefully. "You'll see, George. I promise."

"Move," he barked. He waved the lamp toward the doorway. "But slowly."

Sarah nodded. At first she didn't think she'd be able to put one foot in front of the other. Her knees were shaking, knocking against each other. Nevertheless, she forced herself to step down the hall. Every muscle in her body tensed. George waited for her to pass by him. She nearly brushed against the lamp. There was no telling what he would do. He could very easily clobber her over the head. She could hear him breathing behind her; she could almost *feel* him. She turned the corner into the bedroom—

Aviva!

The girl lay on the floor, gazing up at the ceiling with unseeing, glazed eyes. Sarah knew she should have expected it, but the shock. . . . Aviva's skin had turned a dull blue. Her head lay in a pool of dark brown blood. Ugly purple bruises ringed her neck like a choker. Sarah clutched at the door frame for support. She felt faint. . . .

"Keep going," George ordered.

"I–I . . . okay," she stammered. She hobbled across the dilapidated little room and sank to her knees beside the bureau. *Quickly, quickly.* Her fingers trembled as she reached for Aviva's frayed, overstuffed backpack. With a grunt she yanked at the zipper. An avalanche of damp, dirty clothing tumbled out onto her lap. Sarah's nose wrinkled. The two of them had managed to find lots of shirts and pants on their journey—but they hadn't had a chance to wash any of it. Everything was infested with mildew.

"Take it all out," George instructed. "Let me see everything."

Holding her breath, Sarah furiously dug through their belongings until every last soggy item was strewn on the floor around her.

Wait a second.

Something wasn't quite right. She frowned. One side of the backpack was still bulging. There must be something else inside. She stuck her hand back in and ran her fingers along the nylon lining, feeling for another zipper, another pouch—an *inside* pouch—that Sarah hadn't noticed before. It was strange. Aviva hadn't mentioned anything about a separate compartment. Maybe she wanted to keep some of the clothes they found to herself. But why? Was she embarrassed?

"Take everything out!" George snapped. "I want to see it all."

"I . . . I'm trying," Sarah answered nervously. "But there's something—" Her fingertips bumped against a small fastener, down at the very bottom of the bag. *There!* She fumbled blindly for a moment and managed to pop it open.

"What is it?" George demanded.

"I don't know," she murmured. She stood shakily and turned the bag upside down, letting the contents slide out onto the floor.

A cell phone landed at her feet with a thud. Then a large cylindrical object wrapped in black cloth.

Sarah frowned. What on earth was *that?*

She shook the bag again, just to make sure it was empty.

Something else plopped out: a mottled spiral notebook.

She blinked.

No. That notebook looked familiar. *Very* familiar. It bore an uncanny resemblance to the journal she used to keep—down to the coffee stain on the red cover.

Blood rushed to her stomach. She felt nauseated. It *couldn't* be her journal. Of course not. Her journal was almost two thousand miles away, trapped in a shipwreck under the Verrazano Bridge in New York City—

"Sarah?" George asked impatiently. "What's in that black bag?"

Sarah barely heard the question. She flung the backpack aside and snatched up the notebook, opening it with tingling hands. . . .

To her horror, she found herself staring at her own handwriting.

No. This can't be right.

But the words were there. Words *she* remembered writing. There was no denying it. In a frenzy Sarah slammed the journal shut and tossed it aside, then crouched beside the strange black sack on the floor and tore at the fabric. If Aviva had been hiding Sarah's journal, then there was also a chance she'd been hiding something else. . . .

The cloth ripped.

And in that instant she caught a glimpse of crumbling, yellow parchment and a battered wooden peg.

My God!

A rush of emotions swept over her—they were so overwhelmingly powerful that she could hardly breathe: relief and revulsion, joy and terror . . . but most of all *fear,* a fear so profound, she couldn't comprehend it. The bag slipped from her fingers.

"What the hell is *that?*" George demanded, storming across the room.

"It's . . . it's my granduncle's scroll," Sarah gasped, tears rushing to her eyes. Once again she felt as if she were hearing someone else speak. "It's . . . it's . . . *here!*"

"It's your *what?*"

She tried to swallow, but her mouth was too dry. "It's a scroll. It was written three thousand years ago. In Hebrew. It tells of the Prophecies—the prophecies of the Demon . . . and *me.* Your visions are in there. All of them. It's magic. And there's a code. It's hidden in there somewhere, too. It gives the key to defeating the Demon, but I haven't figured it out yet. . . ." Her voice trailed off.

George didn't say anything.

Finally she looked up at him.

"You were right, George," she choked out, shuddering. "Aviva was . . . she was . . ." She couldn't bring herself to finish the sentence. No. Saying the words would make it real. And it was a reality she was *not* prepared to face.

Aviva was a servant of the Demon. All along she was lying to me, leading me on some wild journey . . . probably taking me straight to the Demon. Straight to Lilith.

Yes. It was so clear now. Sarah had been living alone with her for two months. Traveling with her. Sharing with her. Listening to her. *Believing* in her—

"What?" George asked, glaring at her. "Give me some answers!"

Sarah could only shake her head.

But the fear began to fade. It was replaced with anger, with *rage*. Aviva had exploited her in the most depraved way possible. . . .

Well. There was no point obsessing over it. The girl was dead, and Sarah was glad. George was right. It *was* time for some answers. Sarah ripped the cloth to shreds and gingerly lifted the scroll by its wooden handles, spreading it out on the floor. All the answers were right here, inscribed in that centuries-old black ink. Long-forgotten excitement surged through her system. Her eyes roved over the densely packed Hebrew letters, seeking out familiar words, translating them in her mind as she read from right to left: *The Demon . . . the Chosen One . . . the False Prophet . . . the traitor—*

"That's it!" Sarah cried. The realization hit her like a punch in the stomach, knocking the wind out of her. "The traitor was Aviva!"

"The *traitor?*" George whispered.

She nodded vigorously. "All the Visionaries I met told me that a traitor was near me. *She* was the one. But I was too blind to see it." A hot, bitter taste rose in her throat. "I should thank you, George. You know that? You saved my life." She glanced up at him.

But George didn't seem interested. He was shifting on his feet, drumming his fingers on the lamp. His face was pale.

He no longer looked angry. He looked *scared*.

"What's wrong?" she asked.

"It's just that, uh . . . Harold told everybody that *I* was the traitor. The Visionaries knew about a traitor—and Harold convinced them it was me. He set me up. He used their visions against them." He swallowed, sounding much less sure of himself than he had before. "You said my visions were in that scroll. You said that it was magic. Can you prove it?"

A smile spread across Sarah's lips. She lifted the scroll by its pegs and held it up to George, unraveling a segment of parchment about two feet wide.

"Rip it in half," she said.

His eyes narrowed. "Uh . . . what?"

"Go on. Rip it in half. See what happens."

He hesitated. "Is this a trick?"

"George, you could smash me over the head with that lamp right now," she stated, very calmly. "I'm defenseless. You wanted proof—and I'm giving it to you. If I'm lying, feel free to do to me what you did to Aviva. I mean it."

George glanced down at the lamp. After taking a deep breath, he placed it on top of the bureau. Then he grasped the thick parchment with his grubby fingers and ripped it straight down the middle.

"Like this?"

The two pegs wobbled in Sarah's hands—suddenly free of the tension that bound them together. Without hesitation, she placed them on the floor and carefully lined up the two edges of torn paper, fitting them together like pieces of a puzzle.

"Good," she said. "Now watch."

At first nothing happened.

Sarah chewed her lip. . . .

There it goes!

Once again she felt that jolt of energy, that overwhelming awe of being in the presence of something mystical, something *sacred*. Because gradually, almost imperceptibly, the jagged line that divided the two sides of the scroll began to disappear—as if somebody were wiping it clean with an invisible eraser. The parchment was mending itself, melting back together as if it were made of liquid.

In less than a minute any sign that it had ever been damaged was gone.

"Oh, my God," George whispered.

Sarah smiled up at him.

The color had drained completely from his face.

He took a step back, shaking his head. His terrified gaze darted from the scroll to her eyes and back again.

"You *are* the Chosen One," he breathed.

PART II:

August 2-26

**Trujillo,
New Mexico
Morning of August 2**

Until this moment Dr. Harold Wurf never fully grasped what it meant to be a god.

But as he stood on the cliff, staring out at the sand dunes that stretched to the horizon like pools of swirling caramel, he was filled with a sense of triumph that only a deity could understand. It was a literal *rush*—infinitely more intense than any drug. He could see the future. Somewhere out of that desert wasteland would come a stranger . . . a mysterious girl who would deliver the final key needed to defeat the Demon.

Linda's latest vision had foretold it.

Every element of his victory was falling into place. The troubles of the Promised Land were already fading into a dim past. He felt as if he'd climbed atop a throne to survey a kingdom that would soon be his. And in a very real way, he had. The awesome view was a perfect metaphor for his *achievement,* his fulfillment of a messianic destiny— one that would take him westward and ultimately lead to a triumph over the forces of darkness.

Of course, it also helped that a beautiful blonde was standing at his side.

Linda Altman was a wonder, a marvel. Yes, yes. Such an amazing body. With each passing day of their journey she grew more stunning, more voluptuous . . . so tall and shapely, with those deep, blue eyes that were so much like his own. And she had an intellect to match. *That* was her most remarkable feature. Most of his followers were cretins, mindless sheep. But she *earned* his respect—and very few people did. He was a genius, after all.

"It's going to happen soon," she murmured. "I had another vision this morning. A girl is to come from the east, bearing an ancient scroll. We have to wait for her here."

Harold nodded. But his mind was far away.

She turned to him. "What are you thinking?"

"That I could just stand here forever, looking at you and listening to you speak," he admitted.

She raised her eyebrows. "Americans never get tired of British accents, do they?"

He smiled. That was another aspect of her personality he loved: her sense of humor. "If you'd lived in Texas your whole life, you'd probably feel the same way. Everybody there *tahks . . . lahk . . . thee-iss,*" he drawled.

Linda giggled. "I've noticed. All of you—"

A shower of falling rocks cut her off.

Harold's lips twisted in a frown. So they weren't alone. Leave it to one of his stupid followers to spoil the moment. Hadn't he made it clear that he wanted a few hours of solitude?

He whirled around.

Jeez. He found himself glowering at Julia Morrison.

46

What was *she* doing here? She was supposed to be locked up in a horse trailer he'd brought from his parents' farm. She was dangerous. Those blackouts she kept having . . .

"How did you escape?" Linda demanded.

Julia just shook her head. She looked awful. Her soft brown skin was blotchy. Long dark curls hung in her face, concealing those lovely eyes. And for once in her life, she actually looked *fat*. Yes. Her stomach was undeniably bloated. A round lump protruded from under her dirty white robe. Of course, she *had* been eating a lot. Much more than the rest of the flock. Her eating was almost compulsive, in fact. It was revolting. What had happened to her? She used to be one of his favorites.

"Are you all right?" he asked. He couldn't mask the distaste in his voice.

"I'm fine, Harold," she mumbled. "I, uh, was just, ah—"

"Why are you calling me that?" he interrupted gently. "Why are you calling me Harold?"

She shrugged. Her eyes flashed to Linda. "Because . . . it's your name," she whispered.

"You didn't used to call me by my name." He smiled. "You used to call me what the others call me. The Healer. The Chosen One."

She lowered her gaze.

"You don't believe in me anymore, do you?" he asked. Again his tone was soft. He didn't want to frighten her. No. He simply wanted her to admit to what he already suspected. "That's it. Isn't it, Julia? That's why you were trying to escape."

47

She didn't reply. But he could see a muscle twitch in her jaw . . . and that was answer enough.

"George poisoned your mind," Linda suddenly stated.

Julia's head jerked up. "No. George had nothing to do with—" She broke off in midsentence.

"With what?" Harold asked.

Julia blinked a few times. "Listen, I . . . okay, I *was* trying to escape," she stammered. "But I can't help it. You have to let me go on ahead of you. My visions are stronger than the others'. You *know* that. The pull that I feel . . . I can't explain it. So why don't you just—"

"The flock travels as one, Julia." Harold's voice hardened. "That's something *you* know. We've been traveling west for a week now, and you still insist that *you* are on a special timetable, that *you* have a mysterious need to hurry. Why?"

Her body seemed to wilt.

"It's the Demon, Julia," Linda said gravely. "Either you fight the Demon or you perish."

"Fine," Julia whispered. Her voice broke. She kept her eyes fixed on the dirt beneath her bare feet. "Let me perish, then. Let me just go off on my own. I swear I won't—"

"What will it take to make you believe in me?" Harold demanded, silencing her. "Haven't you seen enough? I drove the locusts from our midst. I *cured* the plague with a touch of my hands. I brought the shower of blood that marked our exodus from the Promised Land. What else do you want me to do?"

Julia just shook her head. Her body began to

shake. Tears fell from her cheeks, splashing softly in the dust.

"Nothing will work," Linda remarked. "The Demon's hold on her is too strong—"

"That's a *lie!*" Julia shrieked. She thrust a finger toward Linda. "You know it!"

Harold cringed. Seeing Julia act this way was so *unpleasant*. She was hysterical, out of control. And he'd had such high hopes for her. But she was clearly beyond any help he could offer. Maybe he should just let her strike out on her own. After all, she would no doubt keep trying to break free from him.

"It's not a lie," Linda said. Her tone was very cold. *"You're* the only Seer who accuses fellow Seers of lying. *You're* the only Seer who feels a tremendous urgency to forsake the Healer. Why do you suppose that is?"

Julia's arm fell to her side. "Linda, please. Just let me go. Please—"

"I'll tell you why," Linda continued, as if Julia hadn't spoken. "Because you have something to hide. You have a secret. *That's* why you want to leave."

"That . . . that's n-not true," Julia stammered. But she looked stricken. She stumbled backward, shaking her head feverishly. "Don't. Don't."

Harold's brow grew furrowed.

He glanced from one girl to the other. Something peculiar was happening here. Linda seemed to be *threatening* Julia. But what did she know that Harold didn't?

"I can't protect you anymore, Julia," Linda murmured. "You've been corrupted."

"Don't!" Julia cried again. "Don't do it!"

Corrupted? Harold shook his head and stepped between them. "Tell me what's going on," he commanded. He glared at Julia. "What is this secret?"

"I don't have a secret," she sobbed desperately.

Harold looked back at Linda. "What's this all about?"

"She's pregnant," Linda answered. The words dripped from her mouth with contempt.

What? Harold's mouth fell open. There must be some kind of mistake. There was no way. . . .

"Pregnant?" he finally snapped. He turned to Julia again. *"How?"*

But the girl crumpled to the ground, howling like an animal.

"It happened before she arrived at the Promised Land," Linda explained in a dry, detached tone. "George is the father. She confessed it to me a couple of months ago. I swore I would keep the secret, but that was before I knew."

"Knew what?" Harold asked. He couldn't stop staring at Julia. His stomach turned. She'd actually had *sex* with that little punk? It was despicable, disgusting.

"Before I knew George had *infected* her," Linda replied. "George was a heretic, a servant of the Demon. His seed was evil. That's why Julia can't be helped. The more that baby grows inside her body, the more she becomes infected with the baby's spirit."

Julia glanced up at them. Her face was wet, twisted with rage. Suddenly she scrambled to her feet. But before she could run away, Linda leaped at her—kicking her legs out from underneath her and pinning her to the ground, facedown.

Uh-oh. Harold winced. This was a little too much. "Just let her go," he found himself murmuring. "We don't want her anymore. Just let her—"

"No." The word was loud, final. Linda shook her head. She was flushed, leaning with all her weight on Julia's shoulders. "We have to destroy her."

Harold hesitated. "What?"

"It's the only way to ensure that she won't destroy *you.*" Linda grunted, struggling to keep Julia under control. It wasn't much of an effort. Julia had lost her strength. She was a pathetic shell of her former self. "If the baby lives, she'll be more powerful than you can ever imagine. You have to burn the both of them to ashes. Only then will your triumph be complete."

I really have to . . . kill her? he wondered.

But he already knew the answer.

Yes. And as much as he might have expected to be repulsed by the idea of slaying somebody once so dear to him, he wasn't. Not at all, in fact. Julia had defiled her body. She had *profaned* it. She wasn't fit to belong to the flock.

Not now. Not ever.

CHAPTER SIX

**Wilderness near Strižhi,
Russia
August 2–4**

The old man called himself "Peek." Or it *sounded* like "Peek."

But that was all the boy knew about him.

As for who he was, or why he was living in this cave, or how he had survived the melting disease, the boy had no idea. Neither did the others. He kept jabbering at them in some guttural language, gesturing wildly at the drawings on the walls. Occasionally tears would well in his rheumy eyes. One moment he would start shouting; the next, he would lower his voice to a whisper. Yet even after almost twenty-four hours, they were still no closer to figuring out *how* he had saved Svetla's life.

They couldn't even thank him.

The next day Peek's demeanor changed. He became quiet, subdued. He spent long periods of time with Svetla, studying the black scars on her skin in the firelight—almost as if making a diagnosis.

Once again the boy could only exchange puzzled glances with Ilya and Misha. What was going on? Was Svetla still in danger? But as if to reassure them,

Peek nodded and smiled. He patted Svetla on the shoulder. Then he scurried to the back of the cave and returned with an armful of blackberries and little pieces of stale bread, which he divided among the four of them.

Finally he pointed toward the cave entrance.

"Allons-y," he wheezed. He began to stamp out the fire.

Smoke filled the boy's eyes. He coughed once. "What's going on?" he asked.

The old man didn't respond. Obviously he couldn't. Instead he picked his way down the narrow passage and out into the sunlight.

Maybe we'll get some answers now, the boy thought.

But when had he *ever* gotten any answers?

In all his travels, in all the many hundreds of miles he had walked, the boy had never hiked so *furiously*. His feet and thighs burned. His dirty clothes were chafing him. How long had they been fighting their way through the wilderness? Three hours? Five hours? And it was fairly clear that Peek had no intention of stopping or even resting.

I should have just stayed in that cave. . . .

The rugged hills had long since given way to a dense, muggy forest. For once Misha, Ilya, and Svetla didn't plow ahead of the boy. They couldn't. For some reason, Peek chose to ignore the established path, leading them instead through a vicious tangle of almost impenetrable brush. The old man's strength and stamina were shocking. Not only did he take it upon himself to clear a passage—hacking at thorns with his bare hands—but he lent Svetla a hand whenever they had to step over a tree trunk or jump a mud puddle. And he hardly seemed winded.

"*C'est près d'ici,*" he kept repeating—whatever *that* meant. What was the point of this? Did Peek even know where he was going? Every turn he made seemed to be decided completely at random. And he was starting to make the boy nervous. Sometimes he would stop for no reason at all, spinning around and holding a finger in front of his mouth to indicate silence. Then he would wait for a few moments and flash that same unreadable smile—

"*Ici,*" Peek suddenly hissed.

The boy stopped in his tracks. His eyes narrowed. Something loomed ahead of them, barely visible through the branches . . . a high stone wall. He couldn't believe it. Who on earth would have gone through all the trouble of building something in *here?*

Without another word Peek dropped to his hands and knees—then slithered into a muddy hole. Misha and the girls frowned at each other. The boy shook his head. Peek couldn't be serious. The hole was only about a foot and a half in diameter.

But one by one, the others squatted down and crawled after him, vanishing into the slimy darkness.

After what seemed like an eternity, the boy pushed himself out of the stinking, wet muck and into the open air. He staggered to his feet and tried to brush himself off, grimacing. He was caked in mud.

Caked in it. That was the last time he would ever fol-
low a total stranger into a hole in the middle of the
woods. No way would he—

Oh, my God. I'm surrounded.

Dozens of people shuffled past him. But they were
seemingly oblivious to the fact that he had just appeared in their midst. He jerked one way, then another. Peek and the others were nowhere to be seen.
The boy's heart pounded. *These people!* Their faces
leaped out at him; he glimpsed a woman who must
have been twice his age, holding a person so small
and fat that it didn't look human. . . . *Baby.* The word
floated up from the dim recesses of his memory. Yes.
A mother and her baby. Only how did he *know* that?
He'd never seen anything like it before. . . .

"Karatyshka!" Misha's voice drifted over the mob.
"Karatyshka!"

The next thing the boy knew, Misha was squeezing him, pounding his back, laughing. But the boy
could only gape uncomprehendingly over Misha's
shoulder at the steady stream of passersby. His breath
started coming fast. None of these people were his
age. None of them. They were all much, much older.
Some of them were bent, limping, *decrepit.* A woman
who must have been ten years older than Peek
lurched in front of the boy's face—gaunt and hag-
gard, eyes buried in the folds of ancient skin.

"Da! Da! Da!" Misha shouted. Then he let go of
the boy, nearly dropping him.

The boy swallowed. *What's going on?* He stared as
Misha ran off ahead of the crowd. Everyone seemed
to be heading toward a thick column of smoke in the

middle of a huge courtyard. . . . The boy could now see that he was surrounded on all four sides by low, nondescript brick buildings. What *was* this place?

He took a tentative step in Misha's direction—when something caught his eye.

Behind the dim haze of smoke, on one of the building walls, stood an enormous painting of a teenage girl in a hooded black robe.

It must have been twenty feet tall. The girl's expression was cold, lifeless, without emotion. And the eyes . . . there were no pupils—only two black holes.

The boy shivered. He felt cold. But it was *hot* in this place. The afternoon sun was blazing down on him. Beads of sweat dripped from his forehead. What was it about that picture that he found so disturbing, so *familiar?* He felt it again—that same uneasy, prickling sensation he'd felt when he'd first laid eyes on the drawing in Peek's cave. He *knew* that girl. He didn't know how, but she was part of his hidden past. A *bad* part. A dangerous part . . .

She's a killer.

That was it! An image flashed through his brain—tantalizingly clear: a group of girls like her, standing outside a house on a rubble-strewn street . . . and they were all armed with machine guns. He was trying to hide from them. But why?

Almost before he was even aware of what he was doing, he started pushing his way through the crowd, straight for the wall. He couldn't tear his gaze from the girl's face. He clenched his jaw. *Somehow* that girl had committed a terrible crime against him. Just looking at her made him feel sick, enraged.

A few people grumbled as he jostled past them, but he hardly noticed. Out of the corner of his eye he saw that everyone in the square was crowding around an enormous cauldron that sat suspended over a crackling bonfire. They were all fighting for a space next to it. . . . He sniffed the air once, and his face shriveled. Whatever was being cooked smelled like dirty socks. But it didn't concern him. No. Nothing concerned him but that girl. He *had* to figure this out. It was so damn frustrating. Why couldn't he remember anything else?

"What does it *mean?*" he cried out loud.

"Dee enemy," a thickly accented voice answered behind him.

The boy whirled around.

A tall, pale guy with short cropped hair was gazing up at the painting as well. He looked about Misha's age. He was wearing green army fatigues. His broad lips were curved downward.

"You speak my language?" the boy whispered.

"Yes." The guy nodded. "Ay leetle beet."

The boy flung a hand toward the girl's face. "Who is she?"

"Dey try to keel every-bah-dee," the guy answered gravely. "Dey send *chuma.*"

They try to kill everybody. . . .

All at once a curtain seemed to part in the boy's head. There was a flood of disjointed memories: He saw a bus, a terrible explosion; he saw himself jumping off a tall cliff into the ocean. And he saw a girl, somebody close to him . . . his *sister.* Yes! *Sarah.* That was her name. It was all coming back. He'd lost her. She had brown hair and glasses, and those girls in the black robes tried to kill her. . . .

". . . neem?"

"What?" The boy shook his head and glanced at the other guy.

"Vat your neem?" The guy pointed to himself. "Mine, Nikolai."

He wants to know my name.

"Josh," he replied. His eyes widened in utter amazement at his own words. "My God. That's *it*. That's . . . that's who I am. Josh Levy."

**Babylon,
Washington
August 7**

Caleb Walker never thought he'd lose his taste for partying. How could he? He basically saw his body as a mechanism for turning his brain to Swiss cheese. It was very scientific. Various alcoholic beverages supplied the fuel. So did a few powders, different kinds of smoke, and an occasional pill or two. This fuel, in turn, fired the pistons that poked holes in the curdled milk of his higher functions: memory, decision making, et cetera. And voilà! He had cheese. From Switzerland.

"Whass wrong, Caleb?" Jezebel slurred. "How come you don't want any more peppermint . . . peppermint . . ."

"Schnapps?" Caleb finished flatly.

He glanced across the food court table. Jezebel had long since given up on trying to support the weight of her own head. She was slumped in front of him, loosely gripping a near empty bottle. One side of her pasty white face was mushed against the gray Formica.

Blecch.

No wonder he didn't want to drink. Jezebel looked

like death. She was breathing loudly through her open mouth, eyes closed. Her long, messy black hair was spread on the table like a shredded place mat. The bright sun streaming down on her through the skylight high overhead wasn't very flattering, either. Nope. It made the pimples on her chin stand out as if they were on display at a museum.

What the hell was he even *doing* in here? It was ten in the morning. On a perfect day. A *normal* day. Everybody else was outside enjoying the summer weather—thankful that for once they didn't have to contend with a freak blizzard, or locusts, or raining blood. He should really take advantage of it. For all he knew, a month-long hailstorm would break out in the next five minutes.

"You dinn . . . didn't answer my question," Jezebel mumbled.

"I quit drinking," Caleb stated dully. "I'm straight edge now."

Jezebel opened one eye, grinning crookedly at him. "Nah . . ."

That's it. I'm out of here. He shook his head in disgust and pushed himself roughly from the table. But even as he stood, his legs seemed to lock in place—preventing him from moving another inch. He knew very well why he was hiding out in Old Pine Mall, why he'd been wasting the days away with *her* . . . the town drunk, the wicked witch of Babylon.

He couldn't face the possibility of running into Ariel. It was that simple. He couldn't deal with seeing Ariel again—not after what he'd heard last Sunday.

62

And the most disturbing thing about it was that he'd gone to Ariel's house to *apologize.* He felt guilty for even *considering* the possibility that she might have killed her own mother. But when he'd walked into that room and seen her on that bed, spilling her guts in a hypnotic trance about dropping a hair dryer into the bathtub . . . *yikes.* He shuddered. Just thinking about it made him want to scrub himself clean—

"Caleb?" Jezebel asked. "Where're you going?"

"Nowhere."

She burped and hiccuped. Then she giggled. "Whoops!" she said.

Caleb scowled. Enough already. He *had* to leave. The chances of running into Ariel were slim at best. No doubt she was still holed up in her house. Maybe he could find a *new* girl to hang out with. One who hadn't killed her mom, and one who wasn't a psychopath. Yeah. He would make that his mission today. There were plenty of single females in Babylon. New kids kept showing up in town, one after another, every single day. It would be easy enough, right? The girl didn't even have to be all that hot. Hell, she didn't even have to speak *English.*

"Siddown, Caleb," Jezebel pleaded in a singsong voice.

"Shut up, Jez."

"You're not going to see *Ariel,* are you?" She groaned.

Caleb swallowed. How did Jez always know when he was thinking about Ariel? But that wasn't even the real question. The real question was, why did it still surprise him?

With a loud sigh Jezebel struggled to sit up straight. Her head ended up flopping back against the back of the chair. She eyed Caleb unsteadily.

"Whassit gonna take?" she demanded.

"What's *what* gonna take?"

Jezebel raised her dark eyebrows. "What's it gonna take for you to see that all those Chosen One freaks are right about your ex-girlfriend? I mean, come on, man. Isn't it obvious? She's the freaking Demon! She's the one they've been talking about—"

"Stop it!" Caleb barked. His nostrils flared. He couldn't listen to this crap—not from her. There was no way Ariel could be the . . . whatever. He didn't even believe in that garbage. It was *sick*. Maybe Ariel was bad, maybe she was downright *twisted,* but she was still a person. A human being. Just like him. Just like Jezebel.

But Jezebel just snorted and shook her head. "I'm only telling you what you already know," she mumbled. "It's, like, pretty obvious. All the Chosen One freaks say that the Demon possessed somebody in Babylon. A girl. Who else would it be?"

"Maybe *you,*" he spat.

"Maybe." A wicked smile spread across her lips. "But I'm not really the obvious choice, am I? Sure, I can *see* things . . . you know, things that other people can't. But I'm not the one who killed my own mom. I'm not the one who makes people vaporize." She laughed out loud, suddenly sounding very sober. "I'm not even Jezebel anymore!"

Not even Jezebel . . . Caleb's face soured. Why did she always say that? What was she *talking* about?

But he knew the answer. She said crazy stuff because she was a total nutcase. Back before the plague, they used to have places for people like her. Yes, sir. Nice places with padded walls and friendly doctors and industrial-strength animal tranquilizers—

"I'm not *crazy.*" Jezebel moaned, rolling her eyes. "I just think we should go ahead and put Ariel out of her misery. Drop her in a bathtub and toss in a hair dryer. An eye for an eye, you know what I'm saying?"

Caleb backed away from her. He bumped against a chair and clumsily reached for another table for support. How could anybody say something like that? Maybe he'd been overly generous when he'd thought of Jezebel as a *person.* She was something else. Ariel wasn't exactly proud of what she'd done. No . . . she was just as freaked out as the rest of them. And Jezebel sure as hell didn't have any right to judge her.

Nobody did.

But that was precisely what *he* had been doing all week.

His throat constricted. He suddenly found that he was furious at himself. Why had he run out of Ariel's house? Why hadn't he asked any questions—to find out if she truly meant to kill her mom, to find out if she was sorry? More important, why was he listening to Jezebel? Why was he even *talking* to her?

Without a word he shoved the chairs aside and ran from the food court. *Leave it to Jez to make me see what a jerk I've been. I gotta get out of here.* His sneakers slapped loudly on the marble floor. *I have to see Ariel. I have to know. . . .*

"You're making a big mistake if you go to Ariel's," Jezebel called after him.

He shook his head. He wouldn't listen to another word. Not one more.

But her voice continued to echo across the vast, empty mall: "Somebody's gonna die there today, Caleb. Count on it."

Puget Drive had never been so quiet.

Caleb stood on the front walk of the Collinses' house, anxiously glancing in either direction down the narrow, tree-lined street. Something didn't seem right. The entire neighborhood was completely deserted. There was a time—not too long ago, in fact—when this yard had been *the* center of town: mobbed with kids, bonfires blazing, booze flowing . . . a nonstop party.

Now it was like a graveyard.

A breeze rustled the pines and the overgrown lawns. The identical suburban homes really *did* look like tombstones, rising up from the weeds. . . .

All right. His imagination was running away with him. Good thing he wasn't on drugs. He looked up at Ariel's cozy little two-story brick house. Her window was dark. But that didn't mean anything. For one thing, the sun was shining, and there hadn't been much power in the state of Washington for about eight months. *Just go up there and knock on her door,* he commanded himself. *It's not hard.*

What was he so scared of, anyway? Jezebel had just been playing her stupid mind games, trying to psych him out. Nothing would happen. Nobody would *die*. Nobody was even *here*. He marched to the door and rapped loudly on it three times.

There were soft footsteps in the front hall.

"Who is it?" a voice whispered.

Leslie. Of course. *She* hadn't ditched Ariel. No—she was a real friend, unlike a certain lecherous alcoholic he knew. He shook his head, disgusted with himself.

"It's Caleb," he answered.

She didn't say anything.

"Leslie?" he called. "Are you there? Can I see Ariel?"

"I . . . I don't know, Caleb," came the uncertain reply. "It's not really a good time."

He leaned forward and pressed his ear against the door. His eyes narrowed. He could hear something . . . a sort of uneven, high-pitched moan—

His stomach dropped. It was Ariel, all right. She was *crying*.

"Look, just—just tell her I'm sorry," he stammered. "Tell her I was stupid for running away from her. I was just freaked out. I want to hear the whole story. Okay?"

Once more Leslie remained silent. Caleb held his breath. He thought he could hear a few hushed mutterings, some more footsteps. . . .

"I can't let you in," an unrecognizable voice sobbed.

Caleb swallowed. "Ariel?" he asked urgently. "Ariel, is that you?"

"Just go away," she begged, sniffling. "If I let you in here, you're gonna catch the plague. I know it. You'll end up like everyone else—"

"Leslie didn't catch it," he pointed out. There was no way he would catch the plague—not after all they'd been through together. Right? He'd been closer to her than anyone else. "Come on. Open up. *Please.*"

"Yeah, Ariel," a dull voice chimed in. "Open the damn door."

What the—

Caleb spun around. *Oh, no.* His ankles seemed to turn to jelly. His pulse tripled. Instantly.

Trevor Collins was standing on the front walk, not three feet away. And so was his fat little idiot side-kick: Barney What's-his-face. Caleb hadn't even heard them. They must have snuck up on him. For all he knew, they had followed him here. . . .

"Surprised to see us?" Trevor asked. He smiled.

Not really, Caleb thought. But he was too freaked out to answer. As much as he hated to admit it, Ariel's brother scared the crap out of him. And it wasn't only because Trevor had once tried to shoot him down. The guy was just so . . . *lifeless.* He talked and acted like a robot. It didn't help that he and Ariel looked so much alike, either. No, their resemblance made him that much more creepy. They both had the same narrow faces, the same brownish blond hair—

"Well, I'm surprised to see you," Trevor said. "I thought you would have kept clear of my sister after . . . you know."

"I—I still think there's gotta be an explanation," Caleb stammered. "Maybe if we all just talk to her—you know, *talk*—we can sort it all out."

Trevor nodded, very casually. "Sounds good." He

peered past Caleb at the closed door. "Ariel?" he called. "Do you want to talk?"

"Go away!" she wailed. "Get out of here!"

Caleb opened his mouth again—but shut it as soon as Trevor took a step forward.

"This is my house too, Ariel," Trevor replied. "I can come and go as I please." His eyes flashed to Barney. Barney shoved a pudgy hand into his back pocket and kept it there . . . as if poised to pull something out.

Uh-oh. Caleb bit his lip. Steeling his nerves, he pushed himself away from the door and planted his body directly in front of Trevor. "Why don't you and me go somewhere?" he whispered, staring directly into Trevor's dead, hazel eyes. "Why don't we talk first?"

Barney snickered. "Because there's nothing to talk about, wastoid."

"I wasn't talking to you," Caleb said slowly. "So why don't you go find an abandoned doughnut shop or something—"

A soft *click* cut him off . . . even before he was aware that Barney had stepped forward and shoved something cold and metallic against his head.

"What was that?" Barney whispered.

All the blood in Caleb's body seemed to pool at his feet.

Well. So much for saving the day. Now he would probably get himself killed—and Ariel along with him.

"Better step aside," Trevor advised. "Barney has a short fuse."

69

Caleb took a step back. "Don't let them in, Ariel. Don't—"

But the front door crashed open, slamming against the inside wall.

"You!" Ariel shrieked, shoving Caleb aside. She thrust a finger at Barney's pistol. "Put that thing away and get the hell out of here!"

Barney shifted his aim to her forehead.

The barrel was less than a foot from her skull.

No. Caleb slumped against the door frame. *Don't. Ariel, please don't.* He stopped breathing. What was she thinking? Barney was a total fruitcake. He'd pull that trigger in a second. . . .

"Easy, Ariel," Trevor warned.

"You want me to take it *easy?*" she shouted. "Screw you!"

The gun slipped from Barney's fingers.

Caleb watched in shock as it clattered on the concrete steps and bounced into the tall grass. What a klutz! The guy wasn't even bending to pick it up. . . . Caleb glanced back up at him. *Oh, no.* Barney's white face was bubbling forth with hideous black blisters. His eyes were wide. He started shaking, then collapsed against Caleb, grabbing at his T-shirt with slimy, blackened, bloody fingers—

"Help . . . me . . . ," Barney croaked.

Caleb bristled. *This can't be happening. Jezebel said that someone would die. She said it.* . . . Horror washed over him as Barney's grasp loosened. The kid sank to the ground and quickly vanished in a steaming puddle of black slime. Caleb had never seen the plague work so fast. In less than ten seconds nothing remained of Barney—nothing but thick, warm liquid that oozed between Caleb's feet, smothering his toes.

Barney was gone.

"You killed him, Ariel," Trevor whispered.

Caleb lifted his eyes.

Ariel was shaking her head. Her skin was colorless. "No," she whispered. "No . . ."

"They're right about you," Trevor said, backing away from her. His voice was trembling. "It's true."

Caleb blinked several times, fighting back the panic that engulfed him like a flash fire. What was Trevor saying? Did he even want to know?

No . . . not really. He couldn't face it. He couldn't stick around. He had to leave. *Now.*

So he let fear and instinct take over. He simply ran. He sprinted across Ariel's lawn and down Puget Drive in the direction of the ocean, as fast as his legs would carry him.

Texas, New Mexico, Colorado,
Wyoming, Idaho
August 8-25

A long time ago I said I
wouldn't keep a diary. This
book was supposed to be a
collection of observations, an
objective journal. It was
supposed to be based on
facts, not feelings.

During the past eight
months, though, I've learned
something. Feelings are just
as important as facts. These
days, they're probably <u>more</u>
important.

I look around, and I
wonder: Where am I? How have
I gotten here? Is it true
that I'm in the backseat of a
stolen blue Chevy, speeding

down a deserted highway with a virtual stranger at the wheel? Yes. But neither of us knows where we're going. We're relying on George's gut feelings and his visions to lead the way. He talks about a mysterious pull that's like a "built-in magnet," drawing him west.

Hopefully that will take us where we need to go. Hopefully.

George says that the Demon will be waiting for us at the end of our journey. But all he cares about is meeting up with his girlfriend, Julia. He figures that as long as Julia follows her visions, they'll end up in the same place. That's what he's praying for, anyway.

I hope for his sake that he's right.

Today we crossed the Texas border into New Mexico.

Nothing changed. I keep staring out the window at the same boring landscape. It's all flat—brown and dead. I'm sure the fields were destroyed by locusts and snow. It's really depressing. I'm starting to go a little stir-crazy.

But George said something that reminded me of my little brother. He looked out at all the flat plains and said, "Who even decides where one state ends and the other begins?"

I don't know why that made me think of Josh. Maybe because there was something so childlike about it—like it just popped into his head, so he said it. Josh always said whatever came to mind, no matter how trivial or pointless it may have seemed to anyone else. It was one of the sweetest things about him. And I know that George is a lot nicer and sweeter than he would like to let on.

It's strange; today was the first time I thought of Josh without getting really sad. I guess I've accepted the fact that he's dead, that I'll never see him again. But I don't know if that's good or bad. I still cry whenever I think of Abrahim. I can't believe I only knew him for three months. It doesn't seem possible. He did so much for me in that short time. He was the one who really made me believe in myself, who made me strong, who forced me to accept being the Chosen One. And I never really got to tell him how I felt.

George says he feels the same way about Julia.

No more dead prairies. <u>Finally.</u> We hit the Rocky

Mountains. The twisty, curvy highways are beautiful up here. My ears keep popping. I can see snow high up on the peaks. It looks the same as it must have looked before the plague—completely unspoiled. The trees are still green. It makes me hopeful, somehow. Even if <u>we</u> don't survive, the earth will, won't it?

George says that we have to start going north now. He keeps zigzagging: north, west, north, west. I hope he knows what he's doing.

We met some other kids today—a group of maybe twenty teenagers living in a small town called Thatcher. It almost seemed as if they were waiting for us. They made us stop and insisted that we take supplies: first-aid materials, food, gasoline, clothing. They said that even in the summer, the Rockies can be treacherous.

So we aren't the first people to be making this journey. Apparently hundreds of kids have passed through here—all searching for the Chosen One, all heading toward this mysterious place in the Northwest.

I don't know whether I find that reassuring or frightening. I didn't tell them who I was. Neither did George.

George is antsy, agitated. He could hardly sit still while we loaded up the car. He says that he knows time is running out, that we have to get there before the Demon strikes. He won't even tell me what he sees in his visions.

Things are starting to get tense. For one thing, George

almost got us killed. He's been driving like a lunatic, gunning the car up to eighty miles per hour on these narrow mountain highways, and we almost skidded off the road. Luckily neither of us was hurt. The guardrail saved our lives. But the right fender is dented, and one of our headlights is smashed.

George apologized, but I could tell he wasn't sorry. He feels he <u>had</u> to drive fast. What can I say? He's probably right.

From now on I'm going to spend all of my time in the backseat translating the scroll into the journal — writing the prophecies down word for word. That way I won't have to look out the window while George drives. That way my mind will be occupied when we swerve off a

cliff and die . . . which at
this rate, we probably will.

But if something _does_
happen to me, there's a
chance that somebody will find
the translated scroll and pick
up where we left off. I pray
that happens, anyway.

Not that I was ever one to
pray.

I can't believe it. I
actually translated something
wrong—a long time ago, back
in February. I guess I was
under a lot of stress—it was
pouring rain in the Sahara
desert and I was starving
to death—but still, it was a
pretty obvious mistake. It's
really ironic, too: the _word_
was _mistake._ I translated it
as _distress._ I don't know
how I did that. They aren't
even close. Maybe it was
because _I_ was so distressed.

The mistranslation got me thinking —because the word was in one of those little nonsense passages at the bottom of every fourth block of text. The passage correctly reads: "Reshape time. In their own <u>mistake</u>, help ends soon. A light is a dear aura. Two twenty ninety-nine."

Two twenty ninety-nine was the day I met Abrahim.

The words still make no sense, of course. But the whole problem made me remember something that Abrahim said right before he died. He told me he thought the code might be hidden in such a way that only I could find it. He said the key to breaking it might lie in the translation —specifically <u>my</u> translation.

I know that everybody interprets things differently. For example, somebody else

might translate "A light is a
dear aura" as "A ray of sun
is a valuable glow." Mine is
closer, but the second one
isn't necessarily _wrong_. So
does the key to breaking the
code lie in my hunch, my
feeling of how those
ridiculous words should be
read?

   And if so, _how?_

   George's visions are
described in the eighth lunar
cycle.
   I read them aloud today,
and he nearly skidded off
the road again. He sees
exactly what is written: the
cliff, the exploding
hourglass, everything. Exactly.
He sees his baby, consumed
in flame.
   He doesn't even _have_ a
baby.
   Neither of us knows what

it means. Is the baby a
symbol for something?

George didn't want to talk
about it. He's frightened. He's
frightened of _me_. And I can't
really blame him.

Sometimes I'm frightened of
me, too.

Yesterday afternoon we
entered Yellowstone National
Park. Nobody is here. It's
the most beautiful place I've
ever been. At sunset the rocky
cliffs turn from gold to red,
and you can see rainbows in
the waterfalls. The fir trees
look soft enough to snuggle
up inside them.

We stopped for the night at
Old Faithful and just sat
there by a fire—watching the
geyser shoot high into the air
every hour or so, splashing
water up above the treetops.
George kept saying how he

thought it was so amazing
that the geyser still worked
just as it always had for
thousands of years, even
though the rest of the world
was falling apart. Some things
never change, he said. Even
when a plague strikes and
blood falls from the sky.
Things like selfishness and
evil and cruelty . . .

I can't believe he really
said that.

He always sees the negative
side of things. I know he
can't help it. It's the way
he was brought up. He lived
in foster homes; he stole; he
hot-wired cars.

So I tried to change the
subject. I told him what I
learned about the Demon—about
how her real name is Lilith,
that she's some kind of
immortal vampire, and that she's
come back to rule the earth.

George thinks Lilith is going to win.

But he doesn't even seem to care. All he really cares about is finding that girl, Julia. He told me that if he doesn't find her soon, then his own life won't be worth living.

And then he just burst into tears. I held him as tightly as I could, squeezing him until he fell asleep in my arms.

He didn't say anything about what happened when he woke up today, but he drove a lot more slowly and carefully.

**Santa Fe,
New Mexico
Night of August 26**

"Burn her! . . . Burn her! . . . Burn her! . . ."

Julia gazed blankly at the frenzied mob. Even now, the situation didn't seem real. She felt as if she were acting out a scene in some kind of sick, black comedy. Everything about it was so cliché—right down to the torches. She was barely conscious of the pain in her wrists as Linda tied her hands behind her back with a rough strip of twine—strapping her body against the trunk of a barren Joshua tree.

How could Harold's flock ever sink so low? She *knew* these people. How would they live with themselves after this?

"Burn her! . . . Burn her! . . ."

The chant swelled to a deafening pitch. It tore through the still desert night—drowning out the crackling flames, the crickets, *everything*. Julia winced as Linda tightened the knot. Knobby wood dug into her back. Her eyes smarted. In the smoke and firelight the sea of leering faces looked inhuman, grotesque. She had a fleeting memory of a book she'd read in a tenth-grade English class: *Lord of the Flies*. It was about a bunch of kids, stranded on a desert

island, who ended up reverting to savagery and trying to kill each other. . . .

Now I know why they made us read it, she
thought. *They wanted to warn us. They knew what
would happen. They knew that if there weren't any
parents or teachers around, then kids our age would
turn into animals.*

Linda gave the knot one last tug, then stepped in
front of her.

"I'm sorry," she whispered. "I wish we could have
saved you."

Julia snorted. Why did Linda insist on keeping up
the charade that she was Julia's *friend?* She didn't
have to pretend anymore. It was over. In a matter of
minutes Julia would be dead. Linda could tell her the
truth now. She could show a little compassion. After
all, Julia *was* very curious. Why did Linda try so hard
to make people believe that Harold Wurf was the
Chosen One? What ultimate purpose did it serve?

"Is there anything you want to say to me?" Linda
murmured.

"Yeah," Julia growled. "Who *are* you, anyway?"

Linda sighed deeply. "That's the Demon talking
again. I know you don't—"

"The *Demon?*" Julia spat. "*You're* with the Demon.
I'm the one who's had the visions of the real Chosen
One. So spare me the lies, okay? We can drop the act.
Just tell me what you really want. Tell me what the
plan is after I'm gone. I'd really like to know."

Linda shook her head.

Then she flashed Julia a quick smile—and vanished into the mob.

You bitch! Julia squirmed in her bonds, tugging at the rope . . . but finally sagged. There was no point in fighting; it would only mean giving in to Linda's twisted desires. Linda *wanted* to provoke her. She wanted Julia to struggle, to scream—to beg for mercy. But Julia would stay strong. She would die with dignity. Even when the flames were licking at her flesh and she couldn't escape . . .

She swallowed. Her heart skipped a beat.

I'm really going to die, aren't I?

"Burn her!"

A few of Harold's mindless flunkies began to lay small, dry twigs at Julia's feet. Her thoughts seemed to condense. *Not much time.* Her gaze swept the crowd again. She caught a glimpse of Luke. His hideously scabbed face stood out from the others like a Halloween mask. He was standing next to that foolish blond girl, Larissa—one of Harold's harem. Julia's insides clenched. Did Harold share his girls with Luke? It wouldn't surprise her. Not in the least. After all, Harold and Luke were very close now. They *needed* each other. Luke was living proof of Harold's powers, of his magic ability to cure the plague—

"Death to the heretic!" Harold bellowed from the shadows. "Let the sacrifice begin!"

Julia bowed her head. Well, Luke finally got what he wanted. She nodded to herself. He always said that if she tried to run away from him, she would end up dead.

And look at me now.

But remarkably enough, even as a few kids stepped forward—eyes glazed, torches held high—

Julia's fear and anger grew distant, fluttering away from her like a leaf on the wind.

Soon she would rest.

Memories of George washed over her in a soothing shower of images: the long drives alone, the carefree days in the cabin, the night after night of lying in each other's arms. . . .

I'll be with you again. Both of us will.

Yes. The three of them would be together for all eternity. She glanced down at the soft bulge of her womb, feeling calm and at peace. In a way, it was a blessing that George had never learned about their baby while he was alive. He had suffered so much already. It would have torn him apart. He had been better off not knowing.

"The flock will be pure from this day forward!" Harold cried. "Purged of lies and deceit! Nobody will ever stop us! Not even the Demon!"

The flames drew closer.

Julia closed her eyes and held her breath. *Please let it go quickly,* she prayed. *Please—*

A sudden pain shot through her spine and hands.

The tree trunk began to shake.

What was going on? Were people jumping up and down? Were they *that* excited to kill her? A deep rumble filled the air. Her bones rattled. She was practically bouncing on the balls of her feet. Her skull smacked against the back of the tree.

"Help!" a voice shrieked.

She opened her eyes. But her vision was blurred; her entire body was *vibrating*. She gasped. Kids were staggering all around her, torches flailing. A few of them tumbled on top of each other. Terrified cries and howls of pain split the night.

Somebody dropped their torch into the pile of twigs at Julia's feet.

Lord help me. . . .

She stared down at the licking flames in horror—when all at once, the earth beneath them split, instantly swallowing the fire into a chasm of empty black space.

Her jaw dropped.

It's an earthquake, she realized. But even before she could make sense of it, she heard a sharp *crack*. The next instant she was being tackled to the ground. *No!* The pain was intense; the impact numbed her almost instantaneously. She tried to scream . . . and nothing came out. She couldn't breathe. She was being crushed, smothered. The tree had fallen on top of her. Her hands were still tied behind her back. She could feel the pressure on her rib cage, pushing her bones to the breaking point—

And then the twine fell free. Inexplicably.

What's this? Her arms dropped to the quaking dirt beside her. Her eyes widened . . . and the tremendous weight slid from her body. The tree was off her. *I can breathe!* For a moment she lay there, sucking in huge quantities of air. Her lungs rose and fell so fast, she thought she might pass out. The ache of bruised bones and scraped skin began to register in her brain.

"Julia!" a voice cried. "Julia, get up!"

Somebody rolled her over on her back.

"Luke!" she screamed.

He was teetering over her, struggling to keep his

balance, eyes furtively roving the panicked mob. "Come on," he whispered, crouching beside her. He nearly fell on his face. "Let's go! Now's our chance!"

"Wha . . . what?" She couldn't understand what was happening. She could only gape up at him, immobilized.

"You're free. Everybody's trying to save themselves. I can get you out of here."

Julia tried to sit up straight. She ended up collapsing back into the dust. Fear coursed through her veins. She couldn't move. She was in too much pain. But she had to get away from Luke. He was lying. She knew it. With every fiber of her being, she knew he wouldn't save her. He would drag her back to Harold and kill her. . . .

But before she could utter a word of protest, he scooped her up in his arms and lurched away from the crowd, scrambling across the trembling desert into the blackness of night.

The Eighth Lunar Cycle

Naamah had never been so enraged.

She felt as if she were losing control—as if she had grasped the spoils of victory, only to watch them slip through her fingers. Lilith's carefully laid strategy was coming unraveled. For the first time ever, Naamah and her sisters had been taken by surprise.

None of them knew about the earthquake.

Naamah didn't understand how such a terrible natural disaster could have been overlooked. Every major catastrophe of the Final Year was hidden in the codes of the Prophecy scroll. And nothing was predicted for the eighth month. Nothing. Naamah should know; she was intimately acquainted with all of the scroll's secrets. All of them. Her ancestors had meticulously copied the entire document thousands of years ago in anticipation of Lilith's return.

She'd gazed upon the copy with her own eyes on the eve of the first attack. . . .

Had her predecessors made a mistake?

Maybe. But even if the Prophecies had been transcribed incorrectly, Naamah could have still prepared for the earthquake—if Aviva had delivered the original scroll to her on time. Naamah could have deciphered the hidden message and made the necessary contingency plans. She could have improvised.

She could have prevented Julia Morrison from escaping.

Yet Naamah wasn't overly concerned about Julia. The girl might be a powerful Seer, but she wouldn't last long in the desert wilderness—particularly with that weak-minded ex-boyfriend. She was lost, pregnant, broken. She would most likely die in a matter of weeks. Her baby would die with her. The baby would never pose a threat to Lilith.

No . . . Naamah was far more concerned about Aviva.

Aviva should have arrived weeks ago. The scroll was still at large. And Naamah couldn't help but suspect the worst: that something terrible had happened, that Aviva was dead, that the scroll had fallen back into the hands of Sarah Levy.

Because if that were true, the Lilum would have to face the unthinkable. Lilith's triumph would be jeopardized. Naamah couldn't afford to wait for Aviva any longer—or even search for her. She couldn't keep stalling. She'd wasted enough time in this desert already.

The clock was ticking. . . .

PART III:

August

August 27-30

Strizhi,
Russia
Morning of August 27

Nearly three weeks passed before Josh could piece together most of his former life. It had come back to him in fragments. Sometimes a single word would trigger a rapid series of memories; other times he felt more hopeless and confused than ever. He spent most of his time alone in the strange courtyard, sitting under the painting of the black-robed girl and running down lists in his mind: *I grew up in New York. I was visiting my sister and granduncle in Israel when the plague struck. I was running for my life and jumped off a cliff into the sea. Misha, Ilya, and Svetla found me washed up on a beach.*

Fortunately, with the help of Nikolai's broken English, he was finally able to communicate with his three companions. He learned that they were medical students studying in Israel. He learned that they had all grown up together in St. Petersburg. So all those months of seemingly aimless wandering were really spent trying to get *home*.

Learning *that* filled him with a nauseating shame. If only he'd known . . . He'd been such a pain in the neck. He was always complaining, always feeling sorry for himself. But even now he couldn't help it. His rescuers were going to make it. He wasn't. *His* home was half a world away.

I'll never see my family or friends again.

He almost wished he still had amnesia.

It could be worse, though. He had to keep reminding himself of that. He had to stop wallowing in self-pity. What was that word Sarah used to call him? A wimp? Yeah, that was it. But at the very least, he had hope. If he stayed in this place, he was certain he would live. He could grow old here—just like the people who queued up day after day in front of that mysterious, steaming iron vat. Just like "Peek" . . . who vanished back into the wilderness without a trace.

Whatever was being cooked up in this place could stop the disease.

Josh had no idea *how,* of course. But he kept watching, every single day . . . watching as the same gnarled old women dumped burlap sacks full of purplish plant bulbs into the bubbling liquid, stirred them for several hours, and ladled them out on a wooden bench to dry in the sun.

By noon the stench of the process filled the entire square. Josh still felt like gagging whenever he took a deep breath. He couldn't get used to the odor. It reminded him of a dirty locker room—only about a thousand times stronger. But nobody else seemed to mind. Not at all. They fought for a space in line, even if it meant choking on that smoke for hours. . . .

"Josh?"

He glanced up. Nikolai was standing over him.

"You should take this," Nikolai said. His tone was stern, serious. *Yoo shid take dees.*

He extended a handful of the bulbs.

Instinctively Josh cringed. Nikolai had never offered the bulbs to him before. Why now?

"Take this," Nikolai repeated. He shoved his palm under Josh's nose.

Uh-oh. Josh's stomach heaved. He clamped a hand over his nostrils. "What . . . what *are* they exactly?" he choked out in a nasal voice.

"Medicine." *May-dee-seen.*

Josh nodded. "Yeah, I figured that. But what is it? I mean, what kind of plant does it come from? What is it being cooked in? And why does it smell so bad?"

Nikolai hesitated. His pale forehead grew creased, as if he were troubled. Then he looked up at the painting and back down at Josh. "You know girls in black, no? You tell me you know girls in black."

Josh frowned. Nikolai had an unnerving habit of changing subjects without warning, particularly if he didn't understand what was being said.

"You see them, no?"

"They tried to kill me," Josh finally answered. "Four of them came looking for my sister. It was back in Israel. They knew about my family and about—" He stopped short. He was about to say *the scroll . . .* but he knew there was no way he could possibly explain it to Nikolai. *He* didn't even know what it was. "But what does that have to do with the medicine?"

"I show you." Nikolai shoved the bulbs into his fatigues. "Come with me. Maybe we learn from each other." He turned and strode across the square toward a building opposite the painting. "Where are we going?" Josh called cautiously.

Nikolai gestured at an unmarked metal door. "I *show* you."

Well. Josh pushed himself to his feet. This was good. He was going to learn something. But for some unfathomable reason, he felt nervous. Why? It wasn't as if he couldn't *trust* Nikolai. The guy had fed and housed him for the past three weeks. He'd given Josh a cot to sleep in, a change of clothes—even a *toothbrush.* Yet Josh couldn't help but imagine that Nikolai would throw open that door—and a bunch of black-robed girls with machine guns would rush out and mow him down. . . .

He swallowed. He was totally paranoid. Obviously his head injury still hadn't fully healed.

As if to reassure Josh, Nikolai flashed a rare grin when they reached the door.

"You are first American to see this place," he said. "It is . . . how you say? Top secret." He yanked open the door with both hands. It screeched loudly—revealing a long, concrete staircase that disappeared down into pitch blackness. Nikolai shoved Josh inside. "I lead way," he said, pulling a small flashlight out of one of his pockets.

Josh paused. "Maybe I should—"

The door slammed shut with a loud crash. Josh jumped slightly. *Why don't I feel good about this?* Nikolai clicked on the flashlight and began to descend. Josh followed wordlessly behind him. Down and down they puttered. It was so *dark.* The steps seemed to go on forever. Maybe this place was a bunker. Or a dungeon . . .

Finally they reached another metal door. It was completely covered in a thick layer of brown, lumpy rust. Nikolai pushed it open. Josh stepped after him—and found himself on a narrow wrought iron catwalk, perched high above an enormous mazelike complex of metal tanks, pipes, ducts, and girders.

Jeez.

Was this some kind of factory? Why had Nikolai brought him here? It looked as if it hadn't been used in twenty years. Low-level fluorescent lighting bathed everything in an eerie bluish glow. Josh leaned forward against the railing and peered at some of the equipment. All of it seemed antiquated and out-of-date: the enormous black levers and dials, the clunky fuse boxes, the mechanical gauges on some of the tubes. And almost every surface was rusted and filthy.

"What is this place?" he asked.

"Laboratory," Nikolai replied. *Li*-borr-*ah-tirry.* "For *jirms.*"

Josh turned to him, eyebrows knit. "For what?"

"*Jirms.*" Nikolai waved his hands. "They make here."

And then it hit him: *germs.*

Oh, no. This place was a weapons factory—for the kind of weapons that annihilated every single living thing on the planet. "Germs are made *here?*" Josh gasped.

Nikolai nodded, very calmly. "Yes. *Jirms.*"

"Are they . . . are they dangerous?" Josh stammered.

"Relax." Nikolai smirked. "*Jirms* everywhere." He pointed a finger at Josh. "Already are in body.

Chuma. You are safe. For now. You are little boy. Medicine is here, also." He dug his hand into his pocket and pulled out the purplish bulbs. "You take, you live."

Josh shook his head. He didn't understand what Nikolai was trying to say. Was he saying that the disease came from this strange, neglected production plant? That this terrible holocaust was somehow *man-made?* That couldn't be possible. "I don't get it. . . ."

Nikolai shoved the bulbs back into his pants. "I show you something in English." He brushed past Josh and shuffled down the catwalk to a metal safe built into the wall. He twisted the dial several times to the right and left. The door popped open—and he removed a stack of yellowed papers. He handed them to Josh. "Read," he said. "Then you know."

> **Communiqué 654 Encrypted 43-Integer Scramble**
> **From: Prophet Ezekiel**
> **To: Mother Bird**
> **Re: Operation Phoenix**
> **Follows: Confirm biochemical production facilities at Strižhi. Germ type unknown. Active bacterial agent attacks hormone glands. Unable to acquire sample. Confirm production of antidote, type unknown. Confirm use of children as test subjects.**

Josh's mouth hung slack. He glanced up at Nikolai. "What is this?" he whispered. The papers trembled in his fingers.

"CIA report," Nikolai replied matter-of-factly. "Very old. Soviet Union capture American spy back in

1970s." He waved his hand for Josh to keep reading. "Go, go. It tell of plan to kill everyone except children. Communists want to take over world."

Communists want to . . . Josh turned to the next page.

Communiqué 771 Encrypted 43-Integer Scramble
<u>From:</u> **Prophet Ezekiel**
<u>To:</u> **Mother Bird**
<u>Re:</u> **Operation Phoenix**
<u>Follows:</u> **Confirm new germ species. Teenagers immune. Repeat teenagers immune. High % of hormones neutralizes bacteria. Confirm plans to smuggle dissemination devices to strategic locations outside USSR. Suspect involvement of KGB and Politburo at highest levels. Antidote type still unknown. Advise bio-haz-mat alert, def-con 3.**

"I . . . I still don't get it," Josh whispered, horrified. He shook his head. "The Soviet Union spread the disease? But why—"

"*Nyet,* not Soviet Union," Nikolai interrupted. "Girls in black. Soviet Union only make *jirms.* But girls in black know about them."

Josh raised his eyes. He shuddered, suddenly feeling very cold. The girls in black knew about *everything.* About his family, about the scroll, about these weapons . . . "How?" he croaked.

Nikolai shook his head. "I don't know." He smiled sadly. "Maybe they capture CIA spy also." He nodded at the pages. "Go, go. More."

Drawing in a deep breath, Josh flipped through the

stack—slowly at first, then more rapidly, and finally in a frenzy. His eyes zeroed on baffling, terrifying phrases: *Devices to be used preemptively in case of imminent nuclear launch. . . . Soviet officials to take antidote. . . . Confirm Soviet plan to institute Communist new world order among teenage survivors. . . .*

The pages slipped from Josh's hands and fluttered to the catwalk grate. He was shaking violently now. Hysteria welled up inside him. "What's the new world order?" he cried, staring up at Nikolai. "What have you *done?* You killed everyone—"

"Nyet!" Nikolai shouted. He glared at Josh, then stooped to gather the papers. "Not us. Girls in black. They attack launch base at Poulostrov Kanin. New Year's Day. I am stationed there. I am only survivor. Devices already placed all over the world. Girls turn key, send signal to devices." He shot Josh another harsh stare. *"Boom."*

Josh ran a hand through his hair. He was sweating. "But how did it happen? The Soviet Union doesn't even *exist* anymore. Wasn't there some kind of treaty banning weapons like this? I mean—I mean . . ." He started pacing back and forth. He couldn't keep his thoughts straight.

"Soviet Union is no more." Nikolai grunted. He stood and shoved the papers back into the safe, then slammed the door. "But weapons are still around. Big mistake, no?"

"Yeah," Josh muttered. "Big mistake." He felt as if he were about to vomit. "So the black-robed girls raided this base—"

"Not this base. Launch base. At Poulostrov Kanin.

This only where *jirms* are made. And medicine. I come here after attack. I want to live."

"Okay, okay." Josh paused, staring into space, stroking his chin. "The Soviets made it here and shipped it to launch somewhere else. I understand that. I understand that they're not responsible. But why did those girls do it? *Why?* What reason could they possibly have?"

Nikolai shrugged. "Maybe same reason as Soviet Union. Maybe they want to start new world order. Who knows?"

Josh blinked. *My God.* Of course. Why else would somebody wipe out most of the population? The girls probably wanted a clean slate—to reshape what was left of the world for their own sick purposes. For all he knew, they wanted to get rid of the *remaining* population, too. Without the antidote survivors like him would be dead in just five years. But that didn't matter. Motives were unimportant. The girls had to be stopped. Period. And the key to stopping them—or at least *stalling* them—was right here, bubbling in that stinking cauldron up in the square.

"How many people know about the antidote?" Josh demanded.

Nikolai stared at him blankly. *"Aynt-tee-dut?* I don't under—"

"The *medicine,*" Josh barked. "How many people know about it?"

"Not many." He shook his head. "No, no. It is top secret. Only people at base, and people who find base . . ."

Josh began pacing again. "We have to start telling

everyone," he muttered. "There has to be communications equipment here, right? We have to send our *own* signal. We have to tell as many people as possible how to make the antidote. It's the only way—"

"*Nyet.*"

Josh froze. "What?"

"If we send message, the girls in black hear. They track signal. They find us."

"Well, you know what?" Josh snapped. "That's a risk we'll have to take."

Nikolai didn't say anything. His face was stony. For a long while the two of them stood under the buzzing blue lights, staring at each other. Nikolai probably thought Josh was going to back down. Not this time, though. No way. Josh was tired of being afraid, tired of being lost and pushed around. He was going to take charge for once. He was going to do something *right*.

"Are you prepared to die?" Nikolai finally whispered.

Josh nodded grimly. "Yeah," he replied. "If that's what it takes, I am."

ELEVEN

**Snohomish,
Washington
Afternoon of August 30**

I'm almost home, Caleb thought, wheezing as he flew down the uneven forest path. *Just a little farther.* His T-shirt was soaked in sweat. His chest felt as if it were on fire. At this rate his heart would probably explode. He didn't care, though. He'd run for another hour. He'd run for another *eight* hours. . . .

Thank God for the National Park Service. They had really kept these trails clear, hadn't they? Even after eight months of neglect, the dirt was still smooth—

His toe struck a tree root.

"Whoa!" he shouted, nearly wiping out.

Okay. He could take it easy for a bit. He downshifted to a stumbling walk. His feet were pretty sore. Anyway, he'd already put maybe twenty miles between himself and Babylon. Possibly more. Three days of walking (marked, of course, by intermittent spurts of panicked sprinting) had brought him pretty far. By nightfall he'd be back in Seattle.

Why did I ever leave?

He shook his head. Looking back on it now, leaving Seattle was possibly the stupidest decision he'd ever made. Nobody there ever talked about Demons or Chosen Ones. And if they *did,* they ended up moving up to Babylon—mecca of the freaks, mom killers, and Visionaries. He never realized how good he really had it back home. Yes, sir. After New Year's Eve life had been a blast: no school, no parents, tons of friends, lots of partying. The only thing he ever had to deal with was an occasional melting or two. Nothing major.

The trouble all started when he met Ariel Collins. . . .

Gradually his lungs began to settle into a regular breathing pattern. He dug into his jeans pocket for a few loose M&M's. It was the last of his food—which was kind of a bummer, being as he was practically starving to death. He really should have thought to pack a bag full of supplies. But his thinking hadn't exactly been clear. He'd spent the last couple of weeks in a stoned haze, hiding out in some random chick's house, desperately trying to avoid Jezebel and Ariel and Leslie and Trevor . . . anyone he knew, really.

He couldn't even remember the girl's name. Merrill? Muriel? Something like that. It didn't matter. What mattered was that she was friendly and that she had tons of weed and vodka. And after *they* ran out—well, so did he.

Caleb shoved a few crumbling bits of chocolate candy into his mouth. He didn't even know why he had bothered to stick around for so long. The smart thing would have been to hightail it out of Babylon right after Barney melted on Ariel's doorstep. No, the *smart* thing would have been to stay clear of Babylon altogether. . . .

Oh, no. Tell me I'm seeing things.

About twenty yards ahead of him the forest came to an abrupt end—and the path stopped. He knew what that meant. Yup. He craned his neck as he trudged forward . . . and just as he suspected, the placid, gray waters of the Snohomish River swam into view.

Great. Now he was stuck. Unless he wanted to swim, of course—which might not be so bad. It would feel pretty good to cool off, actually. He paused at the precipice and surveyed the broad expanse of river. Yeah, swimming this would be no problem. Piece of cake. A smile spread across his face. The tips of a few familiar skyscrapers and the flying-saucer-like top of the Space Needle loomed above the treetops on the opposite bank. He was so close—

"Caleb?"

Jeez! He jerked, nearly tumbling down the steep hill to the water.

"Thank *God* I caught up to you!"

He spun around—and his face twisted into a scowl of disbelief.

It was Leslie. What the hell was *she* doing out here?

"Oh, man," she muttered, jogging to catch up with him. She was wearing a tight black minidress and running shoes. She looked ridiculous. "I'm so glad I found—"

"What do you want?" he demanded angrily. His pulse was still racing from the surprise. "You scared the crap out of me."

She planted herself right in front of him. "I want you to come back to Babylon," she said.

His eyes narrowed. She wasn't even winded. She wasn't even *sweating*—and it was probably eighty degrees. "How . . . how did you catch up to me so fast?"

"I'm not the one who parties all the time." She cocked her eyebrow and smirked. "A lot of people are in better shape than you."

He shook his head. He was too bewildered to be insulted. "Yeah, but still . . ."

"Look, I've been chasing after you all day," she stated. "I followed your tracks in the dirt. I'm *not* gonna let you just bag everything. It's totally irresponsible."

Totally what? For a few seconds he gaped at her. He couldn't believe this. Since when did Leslie use words like *irresponsible?* He almost laughed. This was the same girl who had seduced him in a hot tub with a book of cheap pornography. Was *that* responsible? How was he even supposed to answer her? Maybe he shouldn't. Maybe he should just grab her and toss her off the side of the cliff.

"Caleb, this is—"

"Where do you get off talking to me like that?" he shouted. "You sound like my freaking mother. Who are *you* to decide what I do?"

"I can't decide for you," she snapped. "But I can tell you when you're being a jerk."

He snickered. "Okay . . . *I'm* a jerk?" He jabbed a finger at her and sneered. *"You're* the one who just ran twenty miles for no reason at all. So who's the jerk in this scenario?"

She sighed and rolled her eyes. "You know, you're right. I don't know what I was thinking. If you're happy being a complete wuss and a loser, be my guest."

Wuss and a loser? All right. Now he was more than just a little annoyed. Now he was majorly ticked off. "Um . . . in case you forgot, Leslie, we watched that fat little friend of Trevor's turn into a big puddle of slime. Maybe it's *wussy* of me, but I don't feel like dying just yet."

She looked at him as if he were insane. "You really think Ariel had something to do with that? Is that what you're saying?" Caleb threw his hands in the air, exasperated. *"You're* the one who proved she murdered her mom!" he shouted. "What am I supposed to think? Everybody who gets within ten feet of her bites it."

"You don't," she countered harshly.

He swallowed, kicking the dirt at his feet. "Whatever," he mumbled. He lowered his eyes. "I'm not one of those Chosen One freaks. They're the ones who melt."

"Yeah, well, why do you think that is?" she asked.

We both know the answer to that, he thought. But he couldn't say the words. . . .

"You honestly believe that Ariel is the Demon?"

"Why *shouldn't* I ?" he snapped, glaring at her. "Just tell me that, huh? Give me one reason why I should believe that Jezebel is wrong about her."

Leslie's face softened. "Because you *know* Ariel, Caleb," she murmured. "She's your girlfriend. You've been intimate with her. Do you honestly think she could be some kind of evil being? You know her better than anyone else."

111

"That . . . that's not true," he stammered. "Jezebel and her brother know her a lot better." But he was lying. It was just that he felt diseased, unclean. He *had* been intimate with her. All those nights he'd spent in her house . . . But he couldn't drive himself crazy over it. The past couldn't be changed.

"Yeah, well, speaking of Jezebel, you want to know what *I* think?" Leslie said. "I think *she's* the Demon. And she's been setting Ariel up."

Caleb shook his head. It wasn't as if he hadn't considered that possibility. He couldn't even count the number of times he felt absolutely sure that Jez was the Demon. But that was a long time ago. Nobody ever *died* around her. . . .

"Think about it, Caleb," Leslie went on. Her voice rose. "Really *think*. First of all, the Chosen One freaks say that the Demon started possessing somebody in April. And Barney said that's when Jezebel first started acting weird. So—"

"How do you know what Barney said?" Caleb interrupted.

"Because he took me prisoner!" Leslie shouted. "He kept me locked up in Trevor's compound for a whole week. Remember?"

Whoops. In spite of the fact that Caleb was completely infuriated, he still felt a fleeting pang of guilt. He'd forgotten about that—about how Leslie and Ariel were dragged away after Trevor tried to shoot down all those kids, including Caleb. But he had just run away. . . .

"Anyway, April was when Jezebel started developing all these weird powers," Leslie grumbled. "She started reading people's minds. She escaped from Trevor. And she started saying that she isn't Jezebel. So who is she?"

Caleb didn't answer. He *couldn't* answer.

"Exactly," Leslie said in the silence.

"I . . . I . . . ," Caleb started, but he didn't even know what he was trying to say. He knew how twisted Jezebel was. He knew better than Leslie could even suspect.

"Do you even know what's going *on* back at Ariel's?" Leslie cried.

He shook his head.

"A bunch of Chosen One freaks are camped out in front of her house. They want her to come out— because *they're* scared to go in."

"Can you blame them?" Caleb muttered.

Leslie's mouth fell open. "I can't believe I'm hearing this. Do you know how much Ariel needs you right now? I bet you didn't even know that it's her birthday tomorrow. Did you? Did you? She's gonna celebrate it by herself, holed up in her room."

Caleb rolled his eyes. *Bring on the guilt. Bust out the violins.* This was perfect. Leslie really knew how to push all the right buttons, didn't she?

"All right, forget it." Leslie's jaw tightened. "If you want to let Jezebel pull the wool over your eyes, that's your problem." She turned and marched back down the path in the direction of Babylon. "But I *know* Ariel. And I'm gonna prove to everyone that I'm right. Even if I have to do it alone. You can run away, Caleb. Like you said, it's your choice."

The words ripped through him, slicing an awful

empty hole in his body. *Run away.* He was always running away. From everything. Even when he wasn't actually moving, he was still running away—by getting wasted or by cheating on Ariel with Jezebel. . . . He cringed. How could he have done that? How?

Leslie was right. He *was* a wuss and a loser.

I can't live like that anymore, he realized. *I have to find out the truth—about Ariel, about Jezebel, about everything. Running away won't solve my problems. All this stuff is gonna haunt me wherever I go. Even if something bad happens, finding out will still be worth it. It'll be better than the torture of not knowing. Won't it?*

Maybe it was good that Leslie had chased him down. Nah, he wouldn't go *that* far. After all, he was pretty damn sure something bad would happen back in Babylon. It always did.

But he forced himself to trudge after her, leaving behind the Snohomish River and pipe dreams of Seattle for good.

TWELVE

**Babylon,
Washington
Morning of August 31**

*I'm back on the cliff. Only . . . the night has faded.
It's a new day. I can see this place more clearly than
I ever have in my life. The rocky precipice towers
high over a bluish-green ocean. The coastline
stretches out to my left, far to the south . . . following
the black curve of the highway. I can see the distant,
snowy peak of a mountain in the distance. A pine
forest stands to my right. The trees are so tall, they
seem to poke up into the sky.*

*My baby is in my arms. My beautiful baby with
those magic eyes . . . one green, one brown—so bright,
so powerful.*

*This is where I'm supposed to be. I know it. I've
never been more certain of anything in my life. And I
know that the Demon is supposed to be here, too. The
hourglass is behind me, but I won't look at it. I won't
look when the last grain of sand drops through . . .
when the glass explodes and consumes my baby and
me in flame. I'll keep my eyes on the water.*

"George?" *a voice asks.*

I won't answer. I won't look back.

"George? Can you hear me? George? George—"

"George! Wake up!"

George opened his eyes with a start. He was totally disoriented. His insides were being mushed to one side of his body. . . .

Hold up. He was lying in the backseat of a car. And it was swerving. A lot. He struggled to sit up straight. Sarah was hunched over the wheel, determinedly squinting through her scratched glasses down a narrow, tree-lined road. Her knuckles were white. She kept weaving back and forth across the median lines. Damn, she was a crappy driver. It was a good thing there was no other traffic. She reminded George of the way his foster mom's grandmother used to drive. Like a blind person. Some people weren't fit to sit in that seat—

"I'm really sorry to bother you," she muttered over her shoulder. She stepped on the brake, and the car lurched sluggishly. George's head bumped against the front passenger seat. "But I think you better take over."

"Good idea," he mumbled. He leaned back and nodded. "Yeah. Just pull over, okay? Anywhere is fine—"

They screeched to an abrupt stop, smack in the middle of the road. His head slammed against the passenger seat again.

Jeez.

"I . . . uh, I'm sorry about that," she apologized. She laughed nervously. "I guess it was a bad idea to let me drive. I just thought—you know, you've been doing all the driving, and you looked so tired. I know we're headed in the right direction, so I just thought . . ." Her voice trailed off. She fumbled with the door handle and scrambled out into the sunshine, leaving the engine running and the door open. An annoying *beep-beep-beep* rang through the car.

George chuckled. He rubbed his aching skull. She was a real piece of work, wasn't she? In all his wildest imaginings, after countless visions and blackouts, he never thought the Chosen One would be such a . . . such a . . . well, a *nerd*. It really blew his mind. He'd been expecting some sort of radiant being—a girl who was tall and beautiful and superhuman, surrounded with a glow like the pictures of saints in stained glass windows.

Not plain, mousy Sarah Levy.

Why her? Why is she *the one blessed with all the powers?*

It was just so *weird*—that somebody who looked so meek could perform these incredible miracles. Then again, looks never meant a damn thing. In some ways Sarah was probably the bravest and strongest person George had ever met. About a week ago they were camping when an earthquake struck. They were tossed around like rag dolls. But she remained totally calm. Somehow she knew that nothing would happen to her . . . or to him, either. She kept telling him that he was mentioned in that indestructible scroll, that he was "the most powerful among the Seers." She kept describing his visions. *Exactly*. And she always seemed to know what he was thinking, even before he said it.

Funny. She was a lot like Julia in that way. . . .

Julia. He drew in a sharp breath and squeezed his

117

eyes shut. The old, familiar pain enveloped him, spreading through him like a sickness. *Don't think about her. You'll see her soon enough. She'll get to where she needs to be. She'll meet Sarah sooner or—*

"George? Are you okay?"

His eyelids fluttered open. He glanced up at Sarah through the backseat window. "Yeah," he whispered uncertainly.

She smiled, but her face was lined with concern. "Come take a look at this," she murmured, beckoning to him. She wandered off toward a clearing in the pines on the left side of the road. "I didn't realize we were so high up. The view is incredible."

"Um . . . all right," he stammered. He didn't particularly feel like getting out of the car. As a matter of fact, he would be perfectly happy to lie down and snooze again, to drift back into the dreamscape of his visions . . . to get away from the memories of Julia. But he didn't like to disagree with Sarah if he could help it. She *was* the Chosen One, after all. And she was more than that. She was his friend—the only one he had left.

"You have to check it out," she called.

Sighing, he eased himself out of the car and slammed the door behind him. Maybe a nice, pleasant view would take his mind off his girlfriend. Yeah. The odds of *that* were about one in eight zillion. He sniffed the air as he walked. There was a really crisp, pleasant smell in the wind . . . like salt or something.

He picked up his pace. Sarah had stopped at the rocky edge of a gently sloping hill. *Hmmm.* He glanced around, his eyes narrowing. Something about this little spot on the highway was kind of familiar—

Oh, my . . .

His legs gave out from under him—as suddenly as if he had been struck in the back of the knees with a bat.

Could it be?

He tumbled into the dust. His eyes bulged. His heart was palpitating. *This place!* His head jerked to the right. Those pine trees towering over him . . . he *knew* them! He'd just *seen* them! His gut seemed to rise up to his throat. He felt as if he'd just fallen out of an airplane; it was the same queasy vertigo he always got whenever he slipped into a vision. Only now he was *awake*. He was conscious. He struggled to crawl up the hill.

"Sarah!" he gasped. "Sarah!"

She turned—and her face fell.

"George?" she cried. She dashed to his side and threw her arm around his shoulders. "What is it? What's wrong?"

He shook his head. "My visions," he croaked. His mind was whirling—with fear and shock, but most of all with a tingle of déjà vu so strong that it felt like a thousand invisible needles stabbing into his brain at once. "My visions . . ."

And then he saw it.

The ocean.

He staggered to his feet and leaned on Sarah for support.

"What about your visions?" she asked desperately. "What's wrong?"

But he couldn't answer. He was too overwhelmed,

too fraught with emotion. That body of rippling water, the haze on the horizon, the coastline, even the distant mountain . . . He'd finally arrived home. That's what this was. A homecoming. So much of the past eight months had been spent here, right *here*—on this very cliff. He blinked rapidly. Tears began to flow down his cheeks. He couldn't remember the last time he cried. He clutched at Sarah's shoulder, his body trembling.

"This is the place, isn't it?" Sarah whispered. Her gaze drifted back to the ocean. "This is the place you see in your visions."

George nodded, sniffling. He needed to get a grip. He was acting like a baby. He took a shaky breath and straightened, stepping away from her. Okay. Time to answer some questions. Why was he here? Up until today he'd only seen himself here at night. And where was the Demon? And the giant hourglass? Where was the baby? Whose baby *was* it, anyway?

"What do you think we should do?" Sarah asked.

"I . . . I don't know," he replied. His voice was strained. He swallowed and wiped his face with his sleeve. "There's something—"

Slap!

Something stung the back of his neck. He jerked, scowling.

"What is it?" Sarah asked worriedly.

"I, uh . . ." He shook his head. *Uh-oh*. The pull was back. He could feel it, way down deep in the center of his chest. Yup. It was tugging at him—right between his lungs. He *wasn't* where he was supposed to be. At least not now . . .

Slap!

120

"Ow!" he yelled. *Crap*. That hurt. He rubbed the soft spot behind his shoulder.

"What's happening, George?" Sarah demanded. Her tone was urgent. "Talk to me."

"We . . . uh, we gotta get out of here," he muttered absently. He started shuffling back to the car. He could still hear the *beep* of the door alarm and the soft purring of the engine. "This isn't right. I don't feel like we should be here right now."

Sarah scurried after him. "Why not? Can you explain it?"

"Not, uh . . . not really." He shrugged and slid behind the wheel. "I think we should just keep moving."

For a split second Sarah seemed to hesitate. "Okay," she said. She ran around the front of the car and hopped into the passenger seat. One good thing about Sarah: She never doubted his instincts. Then again, according to her, he *was* the most powerful Seer. Only now he didn't feel like it. Now he just felt freaked out. He slammed his door—then threw the car into first gear and jammed his foot down on the gas.

It felt good to be moving. Very good.

Something bad is about to happen.

He nodded to himself as the car picked up speed. The pine trees rushed past him in a blur. His body sank into the cushions, relieving some of that mysterious pressure under his ribs. All of his feelings seemed vaguely familiar: the edginess, the need to grind his teeth. . . . It wasn't so unlike the way he felt right before he rescued Julia, way back in February.

"Um, George?" Sarah murmured. "Any reason we're driving so fast?"

"Yup," he said. "We're closing in on something." A sign on the right side of the road caught his attention: Puget Drive Next Right. Should he turn? For some reason, he thought he should. The pull seemed to shift. . . .

"Closing in on *what?*" Sarah asked.

George shrugged. "Dunno."

The intersection was suddenly upon him—and he spun the wheel, accelerating. The tires squealed. Sarah fell against his legs. Her head nearly wound up in his lap.

"Jeez!" she hissed.

"Sorry," he muttered sheepishly. He leaned forward and peered out the windshield. Drab-looking suburban-style ranch homes appeared among the pines. The engine whined as the car climbed a hill. His lips curled in a frown. Something important was happening *here?* It didn't seem possible. This street looked like the set for some boring made-for-TV movie. Still, the tightness in his chest told him he was getting closer—

"George!" Sarah shrieked.

He slammed on the brakes.

My God!

The car careened to a stop. George sat still for a moment, panting. Thank the Lord Sarah had said something. He'd nearly plowed into a crowd of kids. There must have been hundreds of them blocking the road, just on the other side of the incline. He shook his head. The steering wheel was damp. His palms were sweaty. He hadn't even seen them coming—or vice versa. They were all standing with their backs to the car.

"Is this what you were talking about?" Sarah said tremulously.

"I . . . I have no idea," he whispered. He rolled down the car window and poked his head outside. "Hey!" he called. "Hey!"

A girl turned around. "Yeah?" she said, looking impatient.

"What's going on?" George asked.

Her eyes narrowed. "You don't *know?*"

George shook his head.

"The Demon's in that house down there," the girl said. A dark smile spread across her face. "You got here just in time. We're flushing her out. We're gonna send her back where she came from. Straight to hell."

THIRTEEN

For the first time since she could remember, Ariel was *not* psyched about her birthday.

Theoretically, of course, it should have been the best one ever. She was eighteen years old. She was a *woman*. If there was a government, she could vote. If things like drinking laws still existed, she could legally imbibe in most foreign countries. But now that the world had fallen to pieces, there weren't any institutions left to ensure that her eighteenth birthday would be special. Today was just as dull as any other lousy day.

Well, except for the angry mob outside her house, waiting to kill her. That was a little different.

Ariel burrowed under her blanket and curled up into a fetal position. She should probably get out of bed at some point. On the other hand, why bother? The last time she'd gotten up (last night? the night before?), she'd walked to the window—only to see several dozen strangers on her lawn, waving knives up at her. No, it was definitely better to stay in bed. She felt so warm and snug, like a butterfly in a cocoon. Didn't she?

Maybe this was all a big joke. Maybe Leslie *hadn't*

gone to search for Caleb. Maybe she had organized a huge surprise party—and all those kids were really waiting for Ariel to step out of her house so they could put on their party hats and blow their whistles and yell, *"Surprise,"* . . . and Ariel would end up raging into the wee hours of the night.

Or maybe Leslie had finally gotten wise and abandoned Ariel, like everyone else.

That was a lot more likely.

Ariel's throat tightened. She sniffed and tried to swallow, but she couldn't. *You're not going to cry,* she angrily commanded herself. *No more. You hate people who cry. You've been crying way too much.*

It was funny. In the past month she began thinking of herself in the second person a lot more. She never used to do that. She never used to call herself "you." *How are you feeling today, Ariel? Pretty crappy, thanks, and you?* It made sense, though. She had to talk to *somebody,* right? And she was the only person left who would—

"Come out here!" a voice outside shouted. "Show yourself!"

A pebble struck the window, glancing off the glass with a high-pitched *ping.*

Ariel frowned. Great. Her adoring public was getting impatient. Didn't people have any manners anymore? She rubbed her watery eyes and sat up straight. *You'll show yourself when you're goddamn good and ready—and not a moment before.*

At least they couldn't *see* her. At least she was on the second floor. If she blocked out all the murmuring voices and stared out at the treetops and the summer sky, she could almost pretend that nobody was there. . . .

"Come out!"

But not quite.

So. It looked as if she didn't have much of a choice. Sooner or later she was going to have to go outside. If she didn't, those kids would probably break down the door. Yup. She had to give the people what they wanted. But that was what she always knew how to do best, right?

The second you walk out that door, they're going to kill you.

The thought crept into her brain out of nowhere—as if an uninvited guest had crashed a party. She knew it was *true*, of course. She'd known it all along. She just hadn't spelled it out for herself in such clear and succinct terms.

Today wasn't only her birthday. Nope. It was also the last day of her life.

The amazing thing about it was she didn't even feel *sad* anymore. The urge to cry had passed. No . . . her dying might be the best thing for all parties concerned.

It wasn't as if she were suicidal or anything. She didn't think she could *ever* take her own life—no matter how bad things got. She was simply doing her duty, facing her enemies, meeting her maker . . . yada, yada, yada. If only people could see how wise and courageous she really was—

My diary!

Of course. She would write her final will and testament. Yes. One last gem for the world to discover. What did people call those things? Epitaphs? *That's* what she would do. And then she would leave this room, this house, and this world for good. A perfect ending to a perfect birthday. She snatched her diary off the rug and found a stray pen tucked into the folds of her sheets.

Dear Chosen One Freaks,

Today, August 31, 1999, I turn eighteen years old. Usually I spend my birthday looking back at other birthdays and reminiscing. For instance, on my seventh birthday Mom and Dad took me horseback riding. It was the last birthday I ever spent with my mom. Maybe that's why I remember it so clearly. It was a blast.

Apparently I murdered her about three weeks later.

But I don't want to be morbid. Not at all. I'm in a great mood right now. I just want to say that I'm sorry for all the mean stuff I did. Like the time I strung Molly Finnegan's bra up on a flagpole because she ratted on me for drinking on school grounds. I feel bad about that, Molly, even though you are a prissy little dork.

Well, that's about it. I can't really think of anything else. I've basically led an exemplary life. Okay, I admit that I'm a little bitter. But I just want you all to know, I am not the Demon. At least I don't think I am.

And if I am, nobody ever told me.
XOXOX,
Ariel

Ariel closed the book with a satisfied sigh. All right. Now she was ready. She stood and laid the diary carefully on top of her pillows. That way nobody would miss it when they came in here and ransacked her room.

Oddly enough, though, her hands felt hot and tingly. Her heart was beating pretty fast. Why was she so scared? There was nothing to be scared of. Nothing at all. If she didn't die today, she would die three years from today. And those would be three very long, very miserable years.

Let's go!

After one last long look at her filthy, garbage-strewn room, she closed the door and headed to the staircase.

Her life hadn't been all that bad, had it? She'd had some pretty good times. Only in the past four months had it really gone down the crapper. Four months out of eighteen years wasn't bad at all. She absently fiddled with her odd metal necklace as she plodded down the steps. Actually, her life really took a turn for the worse the day that Chosen One freak gave her this heinous piece of jewelry. Yet Ariel still insisted on wearing it. Why?

Well, there was no time to answer. She was already at the front door.

"Come out!" the voices shouted. "Come out! Come out. . . ."

"Coming," Ariel answered cheerfully. *This is it! See ya later!* She held her breath and threw open the door—

"Get her!"

Before she could take a single step, four or five kids rushed at her. She didn't even see their faces. All she saw was a flash of metal, bared teeth, and a sea of crazed eyes. She hadn't expected it to happen so *fast*. On instinct she stiffened and closed her eyelids, waiting for the inevitable pain, the first sharp slice. . . .

But it never came.

What the hell?

A gurgling shriek made her eyelids snap open.

Oh, no. Her body went numb. Her vital fluids turned to ice. *No, no!* Every single one of the kids was melting—their features already blackened and unrecognizable . . . dripping, spewing blood, collapsing into heaps of black ooze amid dying screams. Five knives clattered to the ground, swept up in a surge of the muck.

Her attackers were dead.

Just like that. Just like all the others. Ariel was standing ankle deep in their remains. She could feel the slimy warmth on her flesh. She tried to take a step back but couldn't move. Her limbs were petrified. Why was this happening?

"Stand back!" a boy's voice warned. "She'll kill all of us. Remember, she's not of this world. She's the Demon. . . ." The rest of his words were lost in a fit of coughing and gagging.

Ariel lifted her eyes. Some guy was melting on her front walk, not ten feet away.

A terrified wail rose from the crowd. She shook her head.

"I'm not *doing* this," she whispered. "It's not my fault!"

"Run away!" somebody shouted. "Run away. . . ."

A few of the kids began shoving each other, stampeding away from the house. Mayhem erupted on the lawn. Ariel opened her mouth again, but nothing came out. She wanted to stop them; people would get hurt, crushed. . . .

"Wait! I can kill her! She won't give me the plague!"

Jezebel stepped out of the chaos. Her black eyes glittered. She held a serrated carving knife in one hand. It was maybe a foot long.

"It had to be you, didn't it?" Ariel whispered. "You had to be the one."

"Why do you look so surprised?" Jezebel asked, smiling innocently. "You knew that some version of this moment would happen at *some* point. You've known for as long as you've known me."

I guess I have, Ariel realized. A defeated gasp flowed from her lungs. It was true, wasn't it? Their relationship had been one long, jealous, deceitful, hateful war—marked by occasional stretches of phony camaraderie. And this was how it would end. Jezebel would win. After all the mind games and clever double-talk and back stabbing, Ariel was the loser. Her head slumped. She'd never felt more pathetic.

The thinning crowd began to settle down. Some of the people were staring at them now.

"Happy birthday, Ariel," Jezebel murmured.

And with that, she sprang forward and plunged the knife straight into Ariel's chest.

No—

Searing pain shot through her lungs. *The heat!* Her heart was on fire. She staggered away from Jezebel.

But very suddenly, the intensity began to fade. She could feel herself swaying, her mind slipping away . . . the voices outside fading into nothingness. Darkness crept over her, smothering her like a shroud. *I'm dying,* she thought. *This is what it feels like to die.* She grabbed the porch railing to keep herself from falling into the black goo on the floor. But surprisingly enough, her footing remained solid. . . .

She blinked.

The knife was sticking out of her chest.

She stared down at it. Time seemed to slow to a standstill. But she was very conscious of the fact that Jezebel was staring at her, too—with an expression of growing horror.

I'm breathing. Yes. She could see the knife rising and falling. But it was impossible. She must be having some kind of postdeath experience, some kind of hallucination—

"You're still alive," Jezebel croaked.

Ariel gazed up at her, eyes wide. She *was* alive, wasn't she? And being alive was infinitely more terrifying than death.

She grabbed the knife and yanked it out of her chest with a grunt, tossing it to the ground as if it were infected with a deadly disease.

Jezebel started shaking. "You really are the Demon, aren't you?"

I don't know, Ariel thought, panicking. *I don't—*

She bolted out the door and hurtled through the crowd. Nobody tried to stop her. Nobody even *moved.* Everyone was frozen solid. She passed Caleb and Leslie, but she hardly noticed. They didn't seem real. She felt as if she were running through a gallery full of mannequins. Down the street was a car—an old, beat-up blue Chevy. *Escape. Escape. Escape.* The word rang through her head like an alarm. She caught a brief glimpse of some kid with blond hair and bright green eyes standing by the driver's side door . . . and before she knew it, she was shoving him aside.

Close the door, reverse the gear, press the gas—*vroom!*

The car leaped backward. She spun the wheel and skidded out with a screech.

Escape, escape, escape . . .

The ocean was ahead of her. She could see the distant waves on the other side of the pine trees as she tore down the hill. So close. If she just plowed through that little strip of forest, she could fly right out over the water. . . .

Only it might not do any good.

Because when she looked down at her chest, the wound had already closed.

COUNTDOWN
to the
MILLENNIUM
Sweepstakes

$2,000 for the year 2000

5...4...3...2...1 MILLENNIUM MADNESS.
The clock is ticking ... enter now to
win the prize of the millennium!

1 GRAND PRIZE:
$2,000 for the year 2000!

2 SECOND PRIZES: $500

3 THIRD PRIZES: balloons, noisemakers,
and other party items (retail value $50)

Official Rules
COUNTDOWN
Consumer Sweepstakes

1. No purchase necessary. Enter by mailing the completed Official Entry Form or print out the official entry form from www.SimonSays.com/countdown or write your name, telephone number, address, and the name of the sweepstakes on a 3" x 5" card and mail it to: Simon & Schuster Children's Publishing Division, Marketing Department, Countdown Sweepstakes, 1230 Avenue of the Americas, New York, New York 10020. One entry per person. Sweepstakes begins November 9, 1998. Entries must be received by December 31, 1999. Not responsible for postage due, late, lost, stolen, damaged, incomplete, not delivered, mutilated, illegible, or misdirected entries, or for typographical errors in the entry form or rules. Entries are void if they are in whole or in part illegible, incomplete, or damaged. Enter as often as you wish, but each entry must be mailed separately.

2. All entries become the property of Simon & Schuster and will not be returned.

3. Winners will be selected at random from all eligible entries received in a drawing to be held on or about January 15, 2000. Winner will be notified by mail. Odds of winning depend on the number of eligible entries received.

4. One Grand Prize: $2,000 U.S. Two Second Prizes: $500 U.S. Three Third Prizes: balloons, noise makers, and other party items (approximate retail value $50 U.S.).

5. Sweepstakes is open to legal residents of U.S. and Canada (excluding Quebec). Winner must be 20 years old or younger as of December 31, 1999. Employees and immediate family

members of employees of Simon & Schuster, its parent, subsidiaries, divisions, and related companies and their respective agencies and agents are ineligible. Prizes will be awarded to the winner's parent or legal guardian if under 18.

6. One prize per person or household. Prizes are not transferable and may not be substituted except by sponsors, in event of prize unavailability, in which case a prize of equal or greater value will be awarded. All prizes will be awarded.

7. All expenses on receipt and use of prize, including federal, state, and local taxes, are the sole responsibility of the winners. Winners may be required to execute and return an Affidavit of Eligibility and Release and all other legal documents that the sweepstakes sponsor may require within 15 days of attempted notification or an alternate winner will be selected.

8. By accepting a prize, a winner grants to Simon & Schuster the right to use his/her name and likeness for any advertising, promotional, trade, or any other purpose without further compensation or permission, except where prohibited by law.

9. If the winner is a Canadian resident, then he/she will be required to answer a time-limited arithmetical skill-testing question administered by mail.

10. Simon & Schuster shall have no liability for any injury, loss, or damage of any kind, arising out of participation in this sweepstakes or the acceptance or use of a prize.

11. The winner's first name and home state or province will be posted on www.SimonSaysKids.com or the names of the winners may be obtained by sending a separate, stamped, self-addressed envelope to: Winner's List "Countdown Sweepstakes", Simon & Schuster Children's Marketing Department, 1230 Avenue of the Americas, New York, NY 10020.